"Ap kyning, may I enter?"

"It is your ship, captain."

"But you are my—"

Liall gave the man a warning glance. "I would not say that here," he cautioned. "There are no secrets on ships, so they say in Rshan."

Captain Qixa, commander of the Rshani brigantine Ostre Sul, nodded his agreement and stepped into the cabin, closing the door quietly. "That is best." Qixa's pale blue eyes were narrowed, and he rubbed one of his massive hands over the hairless dome of his head in agitation. "I do not know how to begin," he confessed. "There is a matter we must speak of."

Liall stared at Qixa for a long moment, and then took a seat in the only chair available in the cabin. Qixa openly deferred to him in public. Now Liall would see how far that deference went. Liall sprawled in the chair, letting his legs stretch before him comfortably while Qixa stood. "Speak," he commanded.

Qixa took a breath. "When I took you and your... companion... aboard my ship, I was confident in my crew. I thought you would be safe here, at least until we reached the open sea, where anything may happen and where there are pirates aplenty. But now..." Qixa closed his mouth and shook his head.

"Now?" Liall pressed.

"I believe we were betrayed at Khet, before we ever docked at Volkovoi," Qixa said uneasily.

There was a time in Liall's youth when one hard look would have made lesser men tremble for their lives. He let Qixa suffer under that gaze for several moments. "Who?"

Scarlet and the White Wolf Book Two: Mariner's Luck

TOP SHELF
An imprint of Torquere Press Publishers
PO Box 2545
Round Rock, TX 78680
Copyright © 2006 by Kirby Crow
Cover illustration by Analise Dubner
Published with permission
ISBN: 978-1-60370-491-5, 1-60370-491-4

www.torquerepress.com

First Torquere Press Printing: September 2008
Printed in the USA

**If you enjoyed Mariner's Luck,
you might enjoy these Torquere Press titles:**

Scarlet and the White Wolf Book 1: The Pedlar and the Bandit King by Kirby Crow

Scarlet and the White Wolf Book 3: The Pedlar and the Bandit King by Kirby Crow

Windbrothers by Sean Michael

Scarlet and the White Wolf Book Two: Mariner's Luck
by Kirby Crow

torquere Press Inc.
romance for the rest of us
www.torquerepress.com

for J.

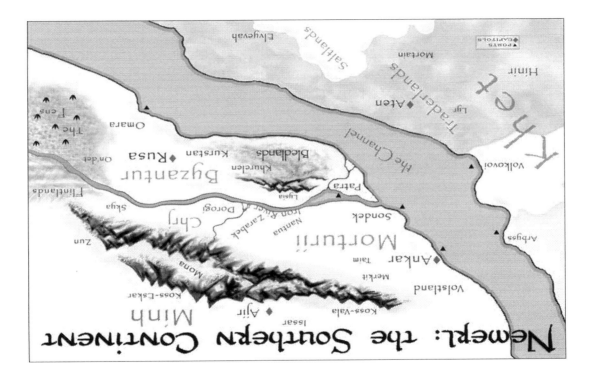

Nemerl: the Southern Continent

Scarlet and the White Wolf

Book Two:

Mariner's Luck

Prologue

One: An Ill Fate

Two: The Mariners

Three: Pursued

Four: Rough Seas

Five: Malice

Six: T'aishka

Seven: The Land of Night

Eight: Nazheradei

Nine: Forgive

Preface

This is the Second Book of SCARLET AND THE WHITE WOLF.

Book One, *The Pedlar and the Bandit King*, told the story of Scarlet of Lysia, a young and honorable Hilurin pedlar, who by chance met a Kasiri bandit on a toll road through the mountains. The Kasiri was Liall the Wolf, a feared and famous giant of a man from the far northern lands of Rshan na Ostre, and a famous atya, or chieftain, among the tribal Kasiri kraits.

Their first meeting was less than polite. Liall demanded a kiss in toll for Scarlet's crossing of the bandit road. Scarlet angrily refused and insulted the atya, and Liall sent Scarlet packing back to his village.

In Lysia, a stranger named Cadan – an Aralyrin soldier in the Flower Prince's Army – began asking questions about the Kasiri blocking the mountain road. Cadan seemed to focus much of his attention on Scarlet, and questioned the young man repeatedly about Liall. The Aralyrin and Hilurin peoples, though sharing a common ancestry, had been waging a sporadic, unofficial war against each other for years, and did not trust each other. Also, the Hilurin have long guarded the secret of The Gift: an ancestral Hilurin ability to use magic. To suddenly have an Aralyrin taking up residence in a Hilurin village and watching the doings of bandits roused Scarlet's suspicions. Scarlet refused to speak to Cadan any further, and angrily ordered the soldier to leave him alone.

For the next several days, as Cadan watched closely, an inventive battle of wills ensued between Scarlet and Liall.

Scarlet tried to sneak by the road in the dead of night, then hidden inside a cart of crockery, and finally dressed in his mother's clothing with his black hair powdered to crone-gray. Liall was fooled by none of it, but highly amused, until Scarlet took the game further and accused Liall of being a brigand and probable murderer.

Enraged, Liall cut the dress from Scarlet and humiliated him in front of the Kasiri. Peysho – Liall's Morturii enforcer – put a stop to it before it went too far, but the damage was done. Scarlet fled down the mountain road, and a regretful Liall followed him.

While escaping the Kasiri camp, Scarlet ran straight into Cadan, who was lying in wait for the pedlar. Cadan attacked Scarlet, meaning to leave his dead body for the village to find and lay the blame on the bandits, but Liall arrived in time to save Scarlet, wounding Cadan and driving him off.

Liall returned Scarlet to his people to recover, and explained to Scarlet that Cadan was a former Kasiri in Liall's krait. Cadan had proved to be more of a brutal outlaw than a Kasiri, and Liall had marked and banished Cadan from his krait three years earlier. Cadan's attack on Scarlet was motivated purely by revenge against Liall.

Deeply ashamed that his actions had put Scarlet in such danger, Liall refused to see Scarlet when he recovered his health and chanced up the mountain road, but granted the traveling pedlar full and free passage through any road that the Longspur krait controlled, forever.

Two months passed. A messenger arrived for Liall from his northern homeland of Rshan na Ostre, summoning the northman on a mysterious quest to return to his family. Scarlet traveled to Ankar, a Morturii city, to work in the souk. There, he made plans to move away from Lysia and join a trade in Ankar, but decided to make one more trip to his village to see his parents and inform them of his decision.

Approaching Lysia, Scarlet could see tall columns of smoke on the horizon. He raced into the village, only to find everyone dead, the homes burning, and the village full of Kasiri. Scarlet assumed that the Kasiri had attacked the village, and drew a knife to attack Liall. Liall protested that that the attack was an Aralyrin raid, bent on murdering the Hilurin, and refused to fight Scarlet. Liall's men disarmed the grieving pedlar, and Liall gently informed Scarlet that his sister, Annaya, survived the raid. She was safe in the Kasiri camp.

Two days passed while Annaya recovered in the krait, tended by her brother, until another survivor straggled into camp: Shansi, the blacksmith's apprentice and Annaya's betrothed. Shansi confirmed that it was the Aralyrin who destroyed Lysia. Liall had his men sifted the ashes of Scarlet's home to find the bones of Scarlet's parents, and Liall helped Scarlet bury them in a peaceful field.

With the seasons turning and Lysia destroyed, the krait prepared to break camp and move back to their base in Chrj. Liall tried to find a way to be alone with Scarlet so that he could investigate Scarlet's willingness to stay with the krait, but Scarlet resisted all of Liall's invitations and the offer was never made. Liall prepared to return to Rshan alone, turning over the leadership of the krait to Peysho, and said goodbye to Scarlet on the mountain road where they first met. Scarlet gave Liall two copper coins – a fair toll for a pedlar crossing a bandit road – and departed with Shansi and Annaya.

A week later, Shansi, Annaya, and Scarlet were settled in Nantua with Shansi's parents. Shansi planned to be a blacksmith there and marry Annaya, and Scarlet was torn between his desire to stay with what was left of his family or to take to the road again as a pedlar. Annaya chided her brother for being a coward and not going after what he really wanted – which was Liall – but Scarlet decided to go with his original plan and return to Ankar.

On the road to Ankar, Scarlet was attacked by a band of Aralyrin soldiers under the command of Cadan. Cadan escaped from Liall with only a broken leg, and was searching the roads for him. A bounty had been placed on Liall's head in every port and garrison in Byzantur by a mysterious Northman, and Cadan believed Scarlet knew where Liall was. Cadan and his men prepared to torture the information out of Scarlet, but Scarlet called on his Gift to escape them, killing Cadan. Scarlet immediately set out for Volkovoi to warn Liall, and also to thwart the vengeance of Cadan's soldiers. In escaping with his life, Scarlet had made also himself a wanted man in Byzantur.

In the meantime, Liall had crossed the Channel and reached the rough harbor port of Volkovoi. There he awaited the arrival of a Rshani ship which would make the long and hazardous crossing through frozen seas, back to Rshan. While walking the docks one rainy night, Liall was attacked and beaten by a pair of club-wielding bravos (hired guards), but saved by the arrival of Scarlet. Two long-knives against two wooden clubs, and the bravos were defeated.

Scarlet helped Liall back to his inn. There, he told Liall about the attack by Cadan and that there was a bounty on Liall's head, withholding the facts of Cadan's death and his own fugitive state. Scarlet asked to accompany Liall to Rshan, but Liall sadly refused, fearing the pedlar would not survive such a long, harsh journey. Too, the Rshani do not tolerate foreigners, and Liall knew that his countrymen would be hostile to Scarlet.

A Rshani brigantine, the Ostre Sul, arrived with the dawn, and Liall met with the ship's captain, Qixa, to book passage. When it came time for the ship to depart, the harbor was guarded by many more bravos on the lookout for Liall. Scarlet distracted the bravos while Liall boarded the ship, and the ship began to leave. At the last moment, Scarlet made a daring leap from the docks with the bravos in close pursuit, dropping to the deck of the Ostre Sul.

The Rshani mariners did not want Scarlet on the ship and were prepared to throw him overboard, but Liall forestalled any violence by promising to put Scarlet ashore to the north, in Ankar. Being no less stubborn than any Hilurin, Scarlet had his own plans about the voyage.

Thus, two very unlikely companions found themselves on the deck of a Rshani ship, enemies behind them, a dangerous voyage ahead, and surely bound for danger. Whatever is to come, Scarlet is determined that he and Liall will face it together.

Scarlet and the White Wolf: Book One : The Pedlar and the Bandit King can be purchased directly from the publisher via http://www.torquerebooks.com

1.

An Ill Fate

The heavy sky was the color of ash, and a light mist seeped from the clouds, covering the flat, soaked landscape in another layer of moisture to add to its endless tides, mildew, sewage, and the constant, pelting rain that deviled the decaying port city of Volkovoi from the month of Trees until the beginning of Wilding. The city was made of many haphazard rows of uneven, ramshackle buildings the color of rotting straw, all jutting up at odd angles, frames sagging against each other for reluctant support. Their crumbling facades bravely faced the waterline, patiently waiting for the inevitable wind or storm that would erase their mark from the scenery. On the pier, a tight knot of leather-armored bravos shook their fists and cursed the departing ship. The crew of the Rshani brigantine ignored the disturbance on land to return to their duties, guiding the great ship northward and home.

Scarlet's skin still tingled with triumph from his near escape from the port of Volkovoi, and he could taste the salt of the air on his tongue. He brushed the grime from his long red pedlar's coat and tried not to appear too smug. He'd gotten away! He was going with Liall! The youth – a slight Hilurin of about eighteen with the characteristic black hair, black eyes, and very fair skin of the Old Tribes – looked up at Liall and affected a casual air.

"I can see this is going to be a long journey. Now, how far is it?" he asked his companion, a towering Northman with hair like snow and icy blue eyes.

Liall frowned. His dark, angular face was the color of amber and he had sharp cheekbones that gave him a forbidding aspect. "You will be put ashore to the north above Morturii, where you should be safe from the Byzan army. You know enough of the language and customs to get by."

Scarlet shrugged. Liall did not sound very convincing, and in any case, it was useless to argue right now. The mariners were watching them with hostility and he had no wish to create a scene that might draw more of their attention. He gave Liall a smile. "You didn't answer me."

"Rshan na Ostre is a four-month journey by sea."

Scarlet thumped Liall hard on the arm. "That's not even a real place!"

Liall laughed, perhaps in sheer surprise. It was hard to tell with Liall. "What do you mean, not real?"

"It's a fairytale. Scaja used to tell me about it when I was no bigger than that barrel there. The Land of Demons, where the Shining Ones live," Scarlet scoffed. "Rshan! Do you take me for a fool?"

Liall was holding his aching arm and chuckling, and Scarlet felt a twinge of guilt for hitting him. The bravos had beaten Liall thoroughly in the Volkovoi alleyway where Scarlet had found him. Scarlet did not know why Liall had been attacked, but he was sure it had something to do with Liall's life before he became an atya of Kasiri bandits.

"I assure you, it is no fairy tale. And it is not called the Land of Demons, but the Land of Darkness, or Night. The words are the same in Sinha, you see. And the commoners in Byzantur just call it Norl Udur, the North Kingdom."

"The North Kingdom is not Rshan," Scarlet said, his patience slipping. He spoke very clearly, as if to the village want-wit. "It couldn't be."

"And just why not? Because you do not believe in Rshan, it cannot exist? That's very arrogant, little Byzan. Even for you."

Scarlet scowled. "Next you'll be telling me *you're* a Shining One." He waved his hand dismissively, highly annoyed. "Forget it, you great ox. If you don't want to tell me the truth, just shut up."

Liall laughed harder as the thin rain gathered strength and became a downpour. And then, to Scarlet's everlasting surprise, Liall seized him, drew him into those big arms, and kissed him passionately. Scarlet went rigid in shock, tense at the sudden feel of strong arms wrapped around him and – oh, Deva! – Liall's mouth on his. Then all his muscles seemed to melt and he moaned and before he quite knew what he was doing, he was kissing Liall back. He sank against Liall's body as the damp wind pulled at their hair and clothes.

Liall broke the kiss suddenly, leaving Scarlet a little dizzy.

"I will always tell you the truth," Liall whispered, his face buried in Scarlet's jet-black hair.

Scarlet felt the tremor in Liall's body and marveled. Am I doing this to him? Couldn't be. His mind buzzed with new questions. It was all too much: the near-fatal episode with Cadan and his soldiers on the road; the narrow escape from the bravos; his dizzying leap from the docks to land on the deck of the Rshani brigantine after Liall had stoutly refused to let him aboard. Now, Liall was hugging him like a lost love. It made his head spin.

Liall's arms tightened hard for a moment. "*Surya*," he added, very low.

"Sunya," Scarlet repeated. "What does that mean?"

Liall cleared his throat and let him go, and Scarlet watched in puzzled amazement as the tall Northman stared out over the waves. Liall seemed to be struggling for control, but over what, Scarlet did not know.

"What's wrong?"

"Nothing, I..." Liall cast a nervous look over his shoulder at the Rshani crew that hovered just out of earshot, casting dark looks at their way. He took Scarlet's arm. "It is the name for the polestar in Rshan, a light to steer by. Come." Liall straightened and seemed to shake off his momentary lapse. "Let us get you out of sight."

Scarlet marked again the intense dislike of the crew as they made their way down the ship, the way they glared at him as if he were a rat on deck. He need not fear mere robbery from them, he surmised, and resolved to stay near to Liall in case one of them decided to pitch him overboard when Liall was not looking.

The crew seemed to sincerely loathe foreigners, which was a pity because he was curious as a cat about them: such large men, so strange-looking, such pale hair and bronzed skin, and such a mighty vessel. Where could they have come from? It had to be Norl Udur, whatever Liall claimed. He wondered where their home port was and where they sailed on their journey, and fought down a surge of frustration at not being able to ask.

Even if you dared ask, he thought, you don't speak their language. He resolved to badger Liall to teach him some on the voyage, which was not going to end immediately north of Morturii.

The Ostre Sul's unsmiling quartermaster met them amidships and led them to a small cabin attached beneath the quarterdeck and the captain's quarters. Like most of the sailors—mariners, Liall called them—the quartermaster wore long leather breeches, oiled to keep water out, and a loose, mid sleeved woolen shirt that seemed to wrap around his waist several times. Scarlet was surprised to see that they wore boots and did not go barefoot as did most sailors he had seen, but winter was coming and he could understand them not wanting cold toes. Their boots were odd: soft-soled like slippers and reaching up over their knees, where they were then turned down like the brim of a hat. Most of the mariners had bronzed skin and long, pale hair that they wore bound tight in a single braid down their backs, but a few had shorter hair like Liall, and one young mariner wore his hair flowing loose. Scarlet thought the style handsome but impractical for a life at sea, and thought the mariner vain. He was also disturbed that the young mariner appeared to slide into hating him so easily. All he had done was leap from the distance from the harbor to the deck of the brigantine and stand at Liall's side, and that seemingly was enough to make the unknown young mariner despise him.

They reached a paneled door below the quarterdeck on the port side and the quartermaster bowed to Liall before leaving them. The cabin was small, but nevertheless both cleaner and bigger than the room they had just vacated above the taberna in Volkovoi. The raw pine paneling of the walls was scrubbed clean, and there was a wide bunk (free of lice, Scarlet checked), and a large cedar chest with a generous supply of padded quilts and thick woolen blankets. Small brass candle lamps hung from the ceiling and one wall. A single porthole, about the size of a plate, opened on the port side. The glass was not uneven and wavy like Byzan glass would have been, but smooth to the touch and clear. There was also a small charcoal brazier attached to an iron pedestal sunk deeply into the wooden planks of the floor. For heat, Scarlet supposed. He fiddled with it a moment and discovered the slitted breathers could be closed and locked to be fireproof, which he supposed might be a necessity in rough water. In truth, Scarlet was simply avoiding looking at Liall. Liall would want to know how Cadan died, and Scarlet's role in it. That was something the pedlar dreaded talking about.

Predictably, Liall started in right away. He dropped his traveling packs on the floor and sank down on the bunk.

"So you killed Cadan. Not intentional, you say. How did that occur?"

Scarlet took a deep breath and related the story: saying farewell to Shansi and Annaya in Nantua, how he was making for Ankar on his own when Cadan and his soldiers caught him on the Common Road to Patra, and how Cadan had revealed that a bounty had been placed on Liall's head,

"They were probably ordered to watch the roads for you. At any rate, I was alone and his men were no better or more honorable than he was, I could see that, and..."

Scarlet trailed off, not wanting to say what had happened next.

"Tell me," Liall pressed.

Liall sat and listened, his mouth flattened into a grim line, as Scarlet related the details of what followed. Scarlet told Liall about the beating, and how he had been terrified of death, and then the instant of fate that he never expected, when Deva herself spoke to him and helped him escape. Why he should have been worth of the notice of the goddess still baffled Scarlet. Who was he but a common pedlar?

"There was a moment when they were careless," Scarlet said, knowing he could not explain how he had called out to Deva or in what manner the goddess had answered him. "I got my hands on my dagger –the dagger you gave me, Liall – and pushed it into Cadan's throat. Then I ran."

"Like a deer, leaving the others alive to tell whatever lies they wished about his death," Liall stated flatly.

Scarlet stared at him. What did Liall expect, that he should have slain them all? He began to say that it was pure chance that the soldiers would let down their guard, that he had his leg bent at the knee, that they in their arrogance did not bother to search him and that his new dagger had been so well concealed in the top of his boot. But he could not say this without renouncing what Deva had given him, and he could not tell Liall the truth. Liall did not believe in gods.

"I... it's like you said," Scarlet mumbled miserably. "I'm no warrior. I ran."

Liall watched Scarlet for several moments, unspeaking. "An ambush," he decided, bringing his hand down on his knee as if pronouncing a verdict. "Those soldiers would have hurt you badly, if not killed you outright. They would have sold you to the Minh at least. You did the right thing."

"I know that," Scarlet replied irritably. "My older brother was taken by the Minh when he was a boy. You don't need to lesson me."

It irked Scarlet that Liall appeared to be passing judgment, even if the Kasiri had found him innocent. Also, he did not want Liall to know how much it bothered him to kill Cadan. Yes, the pig deserved it, but Scarlet still hated how the death made him feel.

Liall looked mildly stunned. "Your brother? I did not know." The matter appeared to trouble him greatly. "What was his name?"

"Gedda," he said, adding hastily; "But it happened a

long time ago, before I remember."

"Oh." Liall paused, thinking. "So... you were telling the truth last night. Your arrival in Volkovoi had nothing to do with me? I suppose going into the Bledlands was out of the question for you?"

Scarlet shrugged and grabbed one of the packs to start rearranging things. "Of course."

"Why?"

Scarlet allowed himself a moment of exasperation. "Deva, you can be dense sometimes! I had enough trouble keeping myself fed with a whole skin on my back in a land that supposedly has law and rule and decent roads. How well do you think I'd fare in the Bled? And, not entirely beside the point, I don't know how to do anything that the Bledlanders consider useful, like raiding or robbing, so they'd only think I was good for one thing. The same thing you thought I was good for when we met."

Liall's gaze flickered.

"I thought I'd take my chances across the Channel," he went on. "It seemed like the only choice at the time."

"Where did you plan to go?" Liall growled. "There are very few Hilurin in Khet. You would stick out like a raven in a flock of doves. If the Flower Prince put a bounty on you, you would be captured very quickly there."

"I know. I thought... maybe beyond the Salt Lands?" He knew he sounded ridiculous even before the words were out, and his voice became snappish. "What else could I do? There's only so many points to the compass. It was either sail to Arbyss or travel east where the Minh would have taken me for their slave or stay where I was and hang."

"You forgot north."

"I'm going north!" he snarled.

A ghost of a smile touched Liall's face, and Scarlet avoided looking at him. He feared he would lose his temper even more and say something truly unwise.

Scarlet examined the room critically. "Only one bed," he said needlessly. It had a large bunk suited to the crew's size, with a thick, feather-stuffed mattress covering the rope frame. He remembered the embrace he had shared with Liall in the inn and wondered if Liall would now want more from him. The thought did not frighten him as it would once have.

Liall shrugged. Apparently, the solitary bunk was no surprise. "And this probably the best they have."

"I'll take the floor," he volunteered selflessly.

Liall snorted. "Do not be a fool. What else are beds for, but to keep the chill of the ground or the deck from reaching a man's bones? And it is going to get very cold, red-coat: colder than you can imagine. You would have lung fever within a week if you were going further than Ankar with me. No, we will both sleep in the bed."

It was the sensible choice, and he was no longer opposed to being close to Liall, but... "The crew will think—"

"What, that you're my slut? They already think that."

He was appalled. "They never."

Liall shook his head, sighing. "My uninformed pedlar, however unfair or arrogant you think me, I assure you, my people are much worse. Living in Byzantur has mellowed me somewhat and disabused me of several bigotries. Listen then, and learn; even a short voyage on this ship will be very hard for you. Rshani do not care for outsiders. In fact, they hold contempt for anyone not of their blood and heritage, for the whole world, perhaps. No Rshani takes a *lenilyn*, an outlander, as a friend. Lenilyn are good to serve, only. Therefore, they will think you my servant, or rather, they see your youth and how pretty your face is and assume what is only natural to assume."

Scarlet's knuckles turned white as he gripped the leather pack. "That I'm a whore."

Liall's face was closed, as if he were holding back a secret, but Scarlet was not shrewd enough to riddle what it was. "Yes."

Yes, and you must swallow it, lad, for what else can you do? Prove them wrong? What use? Whore or servant or friend, you'll still be nothing to them.

It was Scaja's wisdom in his head. Scarlet ached with missing his father, but he decided that the best way to honor Scaja's memory was not to add shame to embarrassment. He got to his feet, squared his shoulders and began to drag items from the pack and place them around the cabin. There was a small table, also bolted to the floor, with a strange, raised rim on its surface. The rim would prevent any items from sliding off in rough seas. Rather clever, when one thought about it. Another low chest with a heavy lid had been provided, and Scarlet began stowing their belongings in there.

"I don't care what the crew thinks," Scarlet said coldly. "As for myself, I think they could use a bath. Several."

Liall slapped his leg, chuckling. "Mariners are mariners, whether Rshani or Hilurin. They all stink."

"This is one mariner who is not going to stink," he declared. "Not with all this water around us."

"It is only water for now. It turns to ice when we leave the Channel and join the northern waters, which you will not see."

"Don't bet on it."

Liall chuckled again and stretched out on the bunk, placing his Morturii knives within reach on the floor. His boots stuck out only a little at the end, so it was a large bunk indeed. Liall wrapped his cloak more tightly around him and sighed.

"I'm just going to close my eyes for a minute," he said,

then yawned. "Wake me if anyone knocks. And do not venture outside the cabin."

Scarlet opened his mouth to object, and then reasoned that he had made enough objections for one morning. He would save some for later. Liall was watching him, one pale blue eye still open to see what he would do.

"I do have my knives," Scarlet reminded him mildly.

"I can defend myself."

"I know."

"And I am no child to be minded by you."

"No."

"I won't leave the cabin."

"Good."

"And I'm not sleeping in that bunk until I have your promise that you'll stay on your side of it," he added mischievously.

Liall yawned. "Given," he said easily, and Scarlet was unwillingly disappointed. He had wanted more of an argument on that point, considering how ardently Liall had pursued him in the beginning. It was not that he objected to waiting, it was just unexpected. After the way his world had turned upside down, Scarlet suddenly felt a keen desire for events he could anticipate.

Liall closed his eyes. In a few minutes, he began to snore softly. Scarlet resisted the temptation to watch him sleep.

The day passed quickly while Liall napped and Scarlet lounged in the cabin, seated on the one large wooden chair, which – unlike the table – was not bolted to the floor. Scarlet felt no small measure of unease about the unknown journey ahead, mingled with a thrill of excitement in his heart: new places, new people, new wonders to see! The promise of fresh horizons never failed to fascinate and distract him. This time, it was a little different, not because he was afraid, but because he felt he had not really chosen this journey. He chose Liall, yes, but the rest seemed more like fate than choice. He wished he had not had to kill Cadan and forsake Byzantur. That was useless wishing, though. It was either his neck or Cadan's, and Scarlet very much wanted to live.

These thoughts occupied Scarlet throughout the day. Liall woke perhaps four hours past noon, yawning and stretching, seeming much recovered from the beating the bravos had given him. They shared a hunk of waybread and some water from the flask Liall carried in his coat. Liall promised to get more from the common barrels stored in the hold, but warned Scarlet that they would have to boil it before drinking.

"It is a ship, Scarlet, not an inn. These men are used to living rough and are somewhat more careless with cleanliness than I would trust my health to. Or yours."

Scarlet was eager to be out on the deck and watch the shore grow smaller as the ship began to make its way northward through the Channel: a long, open body of water between Byzantur and Khet, so wide that one could not see land from one shore to the other. The Channel ran from the warm southern waters of the Serpent Sea to the frozen ice floes of Norl hn, the great North Sea. Liall assured Scarlet that it was not wise to go out on deck, so Scarlet sat there grumbling until Liall heaved an exasperated sigh and promised to let him go above that evening, so long as he did not go alone.

By late afternoon, though, Scarlet had changed his mind. He had not been very hungry all day and the pitch and roll of the ship was making him queasy. He opened the porthole and stood gazing at the waves and the tiny brown sliver of shoreline. Fresh air made him feel a little better, and he began thinking again, about the way the crew had regarded Liall. All these mariners were fair-haired, but none of them had truly white hair like Liall, nor his manners and bearing, which was like a cocksure lord, certain of his elevated place in the world. All of the crew respected Liall, especially the young mariner with the pale, flowing hair who had served as lookout at the port.

That same young mariner came by an hour before dusk while Scarlet was still at the porthole and Liall was again reclining on the bunk. The mariner was a big, handsome man, perhaps five years or so older than Scarlet, and he looked at Liall with clear worship in his gaze. Scarlet was invisible to him for the most part, which was at least a change from the looks given to him by the others. Even the captain had glared at him in dislike. The mariner exchanged words with Liall and left.

"What was that about?"

"Hm? Oh, nothing. Good wishes from the captain, an invitation to dinner later. He was only being polite."

"To you."

"I told you this would not be easy."

True as rain, he had, and here they were not a day away from land and already he was complaining. I'm the one who decided to come with him, he told himself. It won't be that bad.

Scarlet had thought he knew what it would be like on board ship, but that was proven false by the end of the first day. His body had never much liked traveling over water, and he had always experienced a faint nausea when sailing from Patra to Lysia, or even rafting down the Skein River to the Sea Road. By the time the sunset was bloodying the sky, he was hanging over the rail and vomiting into the waves, his strong pedlar's legs turned to rubber beneath him. His weakness was all the more galling because Liall walked sure-footed and without discomfort, while he could only clutch at solid wood and haul his leaden body along. The mariners were surly and unfriendly. The only time Scarlet heard laughter, they were laughing at him: pitiable land dweller, puking his guts out.

"It will pass," Liall said kindly as he helped Scarlet off the main deck. Scarlet struggled against the assistance, mumbling that he could do it himself. Liall ignored his protests and steered the little Hilurin forcibly into the cabin, which had looked comfortable at first but now seemed close and stifling.

"The crew," he moaned, but Liall shrugged.

"A merchant crew of illiterate thugs. Why should you care what they think?"

"Right," he agreed, heaving. There was a bucket near the bunk, and Liall held a cup of water to his lips.

"Rinse out your mouth and spit."

He did and the retching eased. "I think I hate boats."

Liall uncorked a small, brown flask. "It is not a boat, but a ship."

"What's the word for it in your language?"

"Undi'rrla."

Scarlet repeated it and cursed them all, and Liall smiled. "Well, your wit is unshaken if not your legs. It is a good sign. Now; I need you to drink this remedy. It will not taste pleasant, but you must keep it down."

He was not joking. The red syrup from the flask Liall had produced tasted worse than anything Scarlet had ever known, and if Liall had not held a cup of water to his lips immediately after, it would have come right back up.

"I would not," he

advised. "You will only have to swallow it again."

Scarlet tried, swallowing repeatedly and drinking more water, but after a few moments, his stomach rebelled and he hung over the side of the bunk. He looked at the flask Liall held with something like horror.

Liall sighed and shook his head. "No, we will not try it again immediately. In a little while. Next time, hold your nose when you swallow."

Scarlet lay miserably on his side while Liall carried out the bucket to empty. A clean one soon appeared and he held on to the edge of the bunk, trying to lie still. Liall tossed a thick, padded blanket on the floor for himself and left the bunk to serve as a sickbed. Wise of him, Scarlet though blearily. He managed to sleep, chased by unpleasant dreams. Morning brought no relief, either. He started the day off by staggering out of the cabin for a piss, his vision blurry and his head feeling like it was stuffed with wool. He also could not hear very well over the high whine in his ears. The mariners on deck smirked at him as he made his way back, and Liall was awake in the cabin, waiting with the horrible syrup. He did manage to keep it down, but was so miserable afterwards that Liall stayed beside him, wiping his face with a wet cloth.

"You must try to eat something."

He shook his head weakly. "I can't."

"You must," Liall insisted, and pressed a hard chunk of waybread into his hand.

Scarlet sighed. There was sense in that. The oily bread was flat and tasteless, as always. He nibbled at it.

Liall nodded approvingly. "And you must drink, too, or else you really will be ill. If the water disagrees with you, we will try che."

Cold water made him feel worse. "Che," he said weakly.

Liall wiped his face again. "Che it is," he said, then felt

Scarlet's forehead with the back of his hand. He frowned. "Odd. You should not have a fever. You should not be ill this long, either." He rose from the bunk and rummaged in his pack until he found a packet of green che scented with rose. "I will return shortly."

Scarlet nodded and closed his eyes, for even the dim light in the cabin seemed to spear his pupils like shards of ice. To his surprise, he slept again and woke to Liall sliding an arm beneath his shoulders.

His stomach had settled and there was no more of that kind of sickness, though the fever persisted and so did the blurriness of vision and the weak feeling in his legs, so he sipped at the hot che that Liall brought and closed his eyes. The ship rode the waves, lulling him to sleep, but he woke in the middle of the night drenched in sweat clear through to the mattress.

Liall was alarmed and offered him water, forcing him to drink it when he refused, but the water did not make him feel any better, and he sweated out at least as much as he was made to drink. Still, Liall refused to spare him.

Scarlet was not sure when the second day passed into the third; the fever made it hard to remember. Between terrible fever dreams where Cadan cut off his limbs one by one, and the sinister, ponderous sound of the waves crashing against the hull, it was one long nightmare.

Liall became more ruthless on the third day, forcing Scarlet to sit up and drink bitter che while removing the sweat-soaked clothes from him. Scarlet shrank from Liall in embarrassment when the man bathed his bare skin with strong liquor diluted with water, his long hands competent and brisk.

Liall shook his head in annoyance. "You do not have the leisure of modesty at the moment, little one. Come, you must drink," he said, pouring yet another cup of che. "We must get this fever down, or you will die."

At that moment, it was an attractive idea. Then Scarlet dimly realized that they must be nearing Morturii by now. "Aren't you s'posed to be puttin' me ashore?" he slurred.

Liall gaped at Scarlet in astonishment. "In your condition? Alone with no one to tend you? I would be kinder to throw you overboard."

Scarlet almost asked Liall if he would, but sleep claimed him and the morning slipped away in a reddish haze until the older mariner named Mautan, who served as first mate and also as curae to his fellows, came in at Liall's request. The man poked at Scarlet's skin and pinched his jaw cruelly to make him open his mouth so he could peer in at Scarlet's tongue, which earned the man a sharp rebuke from Liall. The mariner stepped back, shook his head and spoke long in an incomprehensible language. Liall's mouth went thin.

"What is it?" Scarlet asked, muzzy with sickness and not really caring. There seemed to be clouds filling the cabin.

"You are very ill," Liall said, his tone uncommonly gentle. "This fellow is telling me what to do for you."

Throw me overboard, he thought and closed his eyes again, for the clouds had begun to take on the shape of ghouls and fanged dragons. When the mariner left, Liall sat beside him on the bunk.

"Can you hear me? Mautan says you are not seasick, but have picked up a fever from that filthy port. Did you eat anything at all there?"

Scarlet shook his head weakly. "Just the waybread and

apples and... yes, the water I steeped the che in."

"Skeg fever," Liall pronounced grimly. A skeg was a type of large river rat that haunted the Byzantur ports. Liall's big hand sought Scarlet's, and Scarlet was surprised to feel it trembling, though he supposed he could be imagining that, much like the dragons.

"The water was hot," Scarlet protested.

"Boiling will not kill this disease. It is not so very dangerous to Rshani, but a little Byzan like you...."

"I'm not little," he managed to moan, swatting at Liall. "The rest of you are just too fucking big."

Liall snorted amusement and smoothed Scarlet's damp hair away from his sweating face. He rinsed out a cool cloth and drew it gently over Scarlet's forehead. "And now you must forgive me, because I intend to make you well again, but it will not be pleasant."

"Oh, 'course not." Scarlet looked up, sweat stinging his eyes so that he viewed Liall through a watery fog. "Tol'... told you I wasn't going ashore," he mumbled, his body slipping heavily into an unhealthy sleep.

"So you did," Liall returned gently.

Scarlet drifted off into a fitful doze, and Liall sat for hours watching over the young man with an expression of worry or grief marking his aquiline features, trying to cool Scarlet's burning body with alcohol-soaked cloths.

An hour past midnight, Scarlet's fever reached its peak and he began calling out to Scaja in a pitiful voice, begging him repeatedly to take him out of the fire. Liall rose and opened the single porthole in the cabin, and the hatch as well, letting the cold air blow through the small space. He stripped Scarlet to the skin and forced him to drink che and water every half hour. There was a fixed look of determination on Liall's face, as if by will alone he could force Scarlet to live.

It occurred to Liall, sometime in the night when the first ugly, violent convulsion rattled Scarlet's slight frame, that he would rather die himself than see Scarlet die. At some point, he had begun to think of the pedlar as his touchstone to his own long-buried honor. Scarlet represented everything good he had lost in life until this point. The arya was not a superstitious man, but if Scarlet died now, on the eve of Liall's long voyage to reclaim his former self, it would be as if a curse had been laid on him.

Not that I do not deserve to be cursed, he thought as he struggled to hold Scarlet down through the worst of the tremors. Scarlet, certainly, did not deserve it. Liall wondered briefly if he should pray, and a harsh bark of laughter escaped his throat. Thereafter, he whispered only small comforts in Bizye, reciting the names of Scarlet's sister and her newly-wed husband, for in Byzantur such chants were used as charms against sickness.

At dawn, the handsome mariner, Oleksei, peered in the open hatch and saw Liall covering the Hilurin with a thin blanket. Scarlet's fever had broken at last, and Liall was weary to the bone and nearly sick himself with relief. Liall turned and snarled at Oleksei to leave them, and the young mariner stared with open shock at the marks of tears on Liall's face before muttering a hasty apology and stumbling away.

"Ap kyning, may I enter?"

"It is your ship, captain."

"But you are my——"

Liall gave the man a warning glance. "I would not say that here," he cautioned. "There are no secrets on ships, so they say in Rshan."

Captain Qixa, commander of the Rshani brigantine Ostre Sul, nodded his agreement and stepped into the cabin, closing the door quietly. "That is best." Qixa's pale blue eyes were narrowed, and he rubbed one of his massive hands over the hairless dome of his head in agitation. "I do not know how to begin," he confessed. "There is a matter we must speak of."

Liall stared at Qixa for a long moment, and then took a seat in the only chair available in the cabin. Qixa openly deferred to him in public. Now Liall would see how far that deference went. Liall sprawled in the chair, letting his legs stretch before him comfortably while Qixa stood. "Speak," he commanded.

Qixa took a breath. "When I took you and your... companion... aboard my ship, I was confident in my crew. I thought you would be safe here, at least until we reached the open sea, where anything may happen and where there are pirates aplenty. But now..." Qixa closed his mouth and shook his head.

"Now?" Liall pressed.

"I believe we were betrayed at Khet, before we ever docked at Volkovoi," Qixa said uneasily.

There was a time in Liall's youth when one hard look would have made lesser men tremble for their lives. He let Qixa suffer under that gaze for several moments. "Who?"

"I have no real evidence," Qixa was quick to say, "but I believe Oleksei knows more of the matter, and he is not stepping forward."

"Then convince him."

Qixa chewed his lip. "There is the problem, ap kyning. I believe Oleksei would have confided his knowledge to me when you came aboard at Volkovoi, knowing who you are and what you stand for. But then you brought the lenilyn with you, and many of my men have taken this very hard. They begin to doubt you. They believe you debase your birthright to suffer this creature in your presence, and worse: they have seen his hand. Four fingers, ap kyning, just as the legends warn. My men believe it is very bad luck. Look at the ill fate that has already befallen the boy."

Liall made a rude noise. "Luck!" he scorned. "A mariner's luck is the sea and the waves and the wind, not a sick, beardless boy lying abed. What harm could he possibly do them?"

Qixa glanced at Scarlet, who lay very still under the blankets, his face pale and his features slack. "There is his magic...." Qixa began.

Liall surged to his feet. "Magic!" he growled. "All of my boyhood, I heard tales of the magic of the Hilurin, and I believed in it. And then I went to live among them. Sixty years and three have I dwelt in the Southern Continent, Qixa, and I have never once seen this magic. It does not exist."

Qixa backed up before Liall's wrath. "That is what they want us to believe!"

"Nonsense!" Liall's arm slashed the air, as if clearing away Qixa's words. For once, Liall did not try to curb his temper. Scarlet had been hovering near death all evening, and Liall was nearly sick himself with worry. "I will not hear this foolishness any longer," Liall shouted. "Are you men or are you children hiding under your beds from the monsters of the night? He is helpless. Can you not see that?"

Unwillingly, Qixa's eyes went to Scarlet again. Qixa studied the boy, seeing the way his chest rose and fell with a halting rhythm and seeing how pinched and pale he was. Suddenly, Qixa was ashamed. He sighed heavily. "There is truth in what you say," he conceded. "This child can do me no harm, but my men do not agree."

"Then it will be your task to you to convince them," Liall returned. Qixa frowned, and Liall saw that the man understood him. "That is my wish," he said with finality.

Qixa bowed his head in deference. "It will be done to the best of my ability, ap kyning."

"Good. And now: this suspect man you spoke of. What is his name?"

"Faal, the sailmaker."

Liall had made a habit of memorizing faces very early in life, and he recalled a slight-framed man with a fine nose and capable hands. "Why do you suspect him?"

Qixa hesitated.

"Speak."

"This man, Faal, disappeared for a day when we were docked at Khet, three days before we came to Volkovoi. When I pressed him, he claimed he went to a woman in the shoretowns, a whore who lives above a taberna."

"What of it?"

Qixa shrugged. "No more, except that it was Faal, and he only has eyes for Oleksei. He thinks he hides it well, the fool."

Liall's smile was dry. "So he chose the wrong lie. Stupid of him. What did you do?"

"I had him strapped for leaving the ship, but not too hard. We still have a long voyage to make and I need his hands in case we tear a sail or – the Shining Ones forbid – lose one. And a woman… it is something any man might do, when the need is on him."

"Even though you knew it was a lie?"

"I knew. The crew did not."

Liall nodded. Qixa did not want to seem like a tyrant to his men, and had gone easy on Faal for their sake.

"Where do you believe he really went?"

"I do not know, but I think Oleksei does." Qixa swept his hand toward the door. "You can question him in my cabin."

Liall glanced at Scarlet. "I should not leave."

Qixa gave Liall an appraising look, and then crossed the cabin to peer down at Scarlet. He moved the covers away and bent down to press his ear to Scarlet's chest, listening. Qixa rose. "He burns, and his heart is weakening."

Liall felt his gut twist with fear. "He will not die."

"But if he is meant to die, whether you stay or go makes no difference."

"It matters to me," Liall said doggedly. "I will not leave. This matter will have to wait."

"As you wish, but I think your lenilyn will not survive the night."

"Do not underestimate him," Liall said, taking a perverse satisfaction in seeing the flash of alarm in Qixa's eyes. "His race brought down the Shining Ones, so far that they have never risen again."

Qixa bowed awkwardly and left. Liall put the chair next to the bunk and sat beside Scarlet. He took the small, fever-hot hand in his own and pressed his lips to it.

"You will not die," he repeated gravely, turning his words into a vow. As he said it, Liall felt a quick and overwhelming surge of weakness in his flesh, as if some of his own strength were flowing out of his bones along with the words. After several moments, Scarlet's fingers tightened around Liall's palm, as if he could sense Liall willing him to live, and he opened his eyes.

Liall shouted a wordless exclamation of triumph as

Scarlet smiled and focused on him. The pedlar's gaze was weary, but lucid.

"You still here?" Scarlet mouthed weakly at him, and then winced as Liall's fingers tightened hard on his hand. "I am here."

Scarlet swallowed and licked his lips, which were dry and cracked. "Thought I was dead for sure," he mumbled, blinking.

Liall did not trust himself to speak for a moment. "You will not escape paying your debt so easily."

Scarlet managed to look amused. "Oh, I'm in your debt again, am I? Figures."

Before Liall could answer, there was a banging on the cabin door and it burst inward. A rush of cold air swept through the cabin. Qixa stood there with Oleksei and two other mariners Liall did not know by name. The mariners held Faal between them.

Qixa entered, and Liall could see the captain was furious. "This one," Qixa growled in Sinha, jabbing a finger at the sailmaker, who was more or less being held upright by the mariners. Faal's face was bloody and his clothes torn.

Liall rose and covered Scarlet with an extra blanket. He shook his head as Scarlet raised a brow in curiosity. "Later," he whispered in Bizye, for Scarlet's ears alone. He turned. "Out," Liall commanded shortly, pushing Qixa ahead of him. He looked over his shoulder to Scarlet. "I will return," he promised before closing the door.

The morning sun was painting the deck amber and gold, and the wind was up: the sails full and the waters choppy. Captain Qixa took Faal by the neck and shook him savagely. The sailmaker's excellent nose was broken, and his pale hair matted with blood. Liall saw that the sailmaker was not much older than Oleksei. Liall stepped closer to Faal, so that the man would have to look up to him. Faal stared at the taller man without fear.

"I know your name," Liall said. "Faal Iannaz. You have family in Rshan."

At this, the sailmaker's posture crumbled and his gaze turned piteous. "You would not harm my family," he begged.

"Why not? You would have harmed mine."

Faal shook his head, struggling with the mariners holding him. "No, no," he groaned. "Only you, it was only to be you."

Liall grabbed Faal by the throat. "Know this: whatever you have done, it was not a crime against me alone. I am my family," he intoned, pulling Faal closer to look into his eyes. "I am Rshan."

Faal trembled and wept. "There was a man in Khet... Aralyrin... he paid me," the sailmaker stuttered, his mouth split, his speech halting. "He gave me your name, and said I should go to a man in Volkovoi and deliver a message if you spoke to our captain or took passage on our ship. I did this."

Aralyrin, Liall thought. Cadan's man, or perhaps even the Flower Prince's. There is no way to know how far the conspiracy stretches. Someone does not want me to reach Rshan alive.

"You are an informant and a traitor," Liall said lowly, amending his tone to one of subtle control. "Who sent this message? Who in Rshan?"

Faal's desperate gaze looked first to Qixa. Finding no help there, he turned to Oleksei, who stared back at him with merciless eyes. "Keep your eyes from me, traitor," Oleksei snarled.

Faal made a choking sound of denial, and then, before anyone could stop him, tore away from the grasping hands of the mariner's and hurled himself over the side into the cold sea.

Qixa bellowed for aid, waving to the lookout stationed above and calling for the sails to be hauled, but it was too late. Nearly half an hour passed before they were able to pull Faal from the icy sea, and he was dead.

Liall spat and cursed as they stood at the rail, Faal's sodden body at his feet, but Qixa only shook his head sagely. "A quicker death than I would have given him," Qixa said. He nodded to the mariners. "Throw him back for the fish," he commanded.

Liall watched Oleksei as the order was given, waiting to see if the man would make any objection, but Oleksei's eyes were flat and emotionless. "Where did he go in Khet?" Liall asked.

Oleksei shook his head. "A woman, he said. I knew it was a lie, but I didn't much care. He was the one after me, not the other way around." Oleksei's mouth curved coyly.

"And then?"

"I found him talking to a man in Volkovoi, one of those stinking half-bloods who guard the port. He wouldn't tell me what it was about. Then you came aboard, and I knew."

"I see." Liall lifted his chin, scrutinizing the young mariner. "So. You are loyal, are you?"

Oleksei bowed his head. "Ap kyning, I am. Humbly."

"Leave," Liall said. Oleksei looked up in surprise. "Your loyalty is noted. Now get out of my sight."

Oleksei backed away before turning and hurrying to the bow. Faal's body made barely a splash as it went back into the sea.

"I wish we could have questioned him," Qixa said, echoing Liall's thoughts.

"It makes little difference," Liall sighed. "The damage was already done. Now we must prepare."

Qixa nodded in the direction Oleksei had gone. "Was

that wise?"

"I do not know," Liall admitted. "He came forward with the truth, but he waited too long. That alone is cause for worry."

"Do you think he knows anything more?"

Liall thought carefully before he spoke, knowing his answer could get a man tortured. "No. If he had known anything, he would have spoken before Faal did, and taken the credit."

Qixa snorted. "You've got him pegged, all right. I know; I've sailed with him for three years. He's always the loudest when it comes to claiming the glory. Well, what of him, then? Shall I have him watched?"

"Not yet," Liall said, his eyes on the horizon, where a thin crimson line separated heaving waters from aureate sky. "He is too clever for that." Liall realized he had not thanked Qixa, and he put his hand on the captain's shoulder. "You are a good man, Qixa."

Qixa's hard smile was filled with pride. "I'm no such thing, but I know my duty." He bowed again. "Ap kyning," he said, dismissing himself. Liall went back into the cabin.

Inside, Liall found Scarlet fast asleep. Liall knelt to feel the pedlar's brow anxiously, and was both surprised and immeasurably relieved to find that the fever had broken.

2.

The Mariners

On the sixth afternoon, Scarlet was able to walk out onto the main deck unaided. He breathed in the salty air and stretched carefully in the dim sun, painfully aware that his muscles were as weak as water and that his hands trembled.

"I was beginning to worry," Liall said. The atya stood quietly at the rail, a landscape of lazy blue swells at his back. The sky was pale and almost colorless.

"Surely not," Scarlet replied wanly. "I'm a redbird, remember? Tough as shoe leather."

"Oh, I never forgot."

As they made their way back to the cabin, Scarlet spied a handsome young mariner waving at Liall from the rigging high above. Scarlet recognized him as the lookout who always seemed to have his eyes on Liall. "What is that man's name?" Scarlet asked, trying to appear indifferent. "The young one who looks at you so often."

"Oleksei," Liall said, and gave the mariner a casual nod. Scarlet nearly nodded at him, too, but then he saw Oleksei pinning him with an idle stare of contempt. The man turned aside to say something to one of his shipmates, who grinned darkly and cast measuring stares his way.

"They really don't like me," Scarlet muttered.

"My people are not fond of foreigners, as I have said."

"A pox on your people."

Liall chuckled and ruffled Scarlet's hair, which earned Scarlet another hate-filled glare from Oleksei.

Back in the cabin, Scarlet fell into the bunk and slept the night away. The seventh day dawned and the fever did not return. He slept heavily and ate several bowls of fish broth and some waybread. Thereafter, the sickness departed and it seemed that Scarlet had found his sea legs. Liall quit his pallet on the floor and joined Scarlet in the bunk, though he was careful to keep a few inches between them and they had separate blankets. He did not mention putting Scarlet ashore again, and it seemed that the journey would, after all, settle into the dull monotony of travel. With luck, the rest of the trip would be uneventful.

"I told you it was not seasickness," Liall said cheerfully on the tenth day, right after Scarlet lost his breakfast over the rail. "*This* is seasickness."

"Bastard," Scarlet muttered, spitting into the water, which was white-capped and slamming against the hull. Rough seas had brought on the nausea, but he weathered it a lot better on an empty stomach. Scarlet wiped his mouth with his sleeve and wished for a bath. For the first few days after being ill, he had come out on deck to wash his hands and face and clean his clothing as best as he could, but the mariners had stared the first day and by the second it was a spectacle, with a knot of them standing around and grinning at him as he washed. He took to washing up in the cabin alone after that. Liall let the change pass without comment, but every morning there was now a clean bucket of water in the cabin. Not being a sailor, it did not occur right away to Scarlet how precious fresh water was at sea, so it was a long while before he could fully appreciate the kindness.

"You are looking better, too," Liall commented. "There is color in your face again, and you have no bruised look beneath your eyes."

Scarlet knew he had lost some weight and looked thin and unwell compared to all these strong, hale men on board, especially Oleksei. He glanced up at Liall, feeling suddenly embarrassed. "Thank you," he said awkwardly.

"Whatever for?"

"For taking care of me when I was ill."

Liall gave Scarlet one of his mocking looks. "My motives are entirely selfish. I enjoy your company."

Scarlet and spat again into the water. "Such as it is." He smiled uncertainly at Liall, knowing that his clothes needed a good wash and that his hair was unkempt and his nails grimy. Liall, on the other hand, was as imposing as ever in a long black cloak with hood and gray woolen breeches and new boots. The cloak was embroidered with silver and blue at the edges and had a sturdy gold clasp at his throat in the shape of a crouching bear. He was sure that Liall would draw looks in any crowd, and he suddenly felt grubby and small beside him, like a plain-feathered robin gazing up at an eagle.

Scarlet realized he was staring. Liall's mouth curved and he reached out to stroke Scarlet's unruly hair into place.

"What are you thinking, redbird?"

"Nothing," he replied quickly, and felt his face heating up.

Mautan the mate appeared and said something to Liall. Liall nodded to Mautan and spoke a few words in scratchy Sinha, a language that must be spoken in the back of the throat to get it right. The mate moved away with a rolling, sailor's stride that utterly nullified the swaying of the deck, looking as steady as a goat wandering along a flat path. Liall could do this, too, but so far the trick had eluded Scarlet.

"I must speak with the captain now," Liall said. "Stay here in the sun for a bit; the fresh air will do you good."

Scarlet nodded. His strength was far from fully returned, and now his legs felt wobbly again and he was not ready to try breakfast again so soon after losing the first. Liall patted him on the shoulder and followed the mariner in the direction of the captain's cabin.

Scarlet watched him walk away and wished he knew more about Liall, about his family and why his presence was needed so urgently. He still did not really believe that Liall's country was the fairytale land of Rshan, and he was annoyed that every time he badgered Liall for details on his family, Liall would reply that it was too dangerous for him to know more than the barest information. The atya had offered to make up a charming lie, which irritated Scarlet so much that he refused to talk to him for the remainder of one evening. Too dangerous, indeed! Never mind that *he* had saved Liall's skin on arriving in Volkovoi, and that he had cleared the bravos so they could board the ship; it was too dangerous. Still, Liall seemed to believe what he was saying.

Tilting his face up into the wind, Scarlet closed his eyes and breathed the salt air, trying to be patient. Liall had been right about the fever and he had been right about being able to cure him of it, so perhaps he was right about Rshan. Yet, it bothered Scarlet's fierce sense of independence to be relying so much on someone else.

Scarlet's eyes flew open as a spate of Sinha near his ear startled him, and he turned to see a mariner he did not recognize standing quite close to his side. The blond mariner was grinning and Scarlet saw he had lost an eyetooth in some dockside battle or to scurvy.

"Sorry, I don't understand," he said.

The mariner held up a silver bit and gestured, miming handing the coin to someone else.

No wiser, Scarlet looked over his shoulder, hoping to see Liall, but no luck there. He shrugged.

Still grinning, the man gripped the front of Scarlet's shirt and dropped the coin inside.

His jaw dropped. "What—" Scarlet began, but the mariner took hold of Scarlet's wrist and pressed the pedlar's hand firmly against his groin.

Shock held him immobile for a moment. He jerked his hand away, fumbled the coin out, and flung it at the mariner.

"Sheep-raping, dung-eating maggot!" he shouted and swung his fist. It connected solidly on target with the mariner's jaw, and the man staggered back. By the time Liall blessedly reappeared with the captain, Scarlet was shaking his numb hand and surrounded by angry, shouting mariners.

Scarlet was small and the mariner nearly twice his size, but the mariner was flat on the deck, holding his jaw. Neither the captain nor Liall seemed particularly impressed by this. Liall fixed Scarlet with a grim look.

"What happened?"

Scarlet told him the bare facts: "He tried to buy me into his bed."

"How?"

"He put a coin down my shirt and put my hand on him."

"So you punched him?"

"Yes!"

Liall was exasperated. "For Deva's sake, you can be such a child. Why not just return the coin?" Liall turned to the captain and began explaining.

Scarlet was coldly furious. He steadied himself against the rail while the offending mariner stood glaring. The man gave Scarlet a bleary look that held hatred, and Scarlet saw Oleksei smirking at him with satisfaction. He suddenly felt cold and alone.

Captain Qixa began speaking to his crew, his tone sharp. Liall spoke to Qixa and then to the mariner Scarlet had punched, his tone mild and humorous.

"What are you saying?" Scarlet demanded. "Don't apologize for me."

Liall turned on him. "*Silence!*" he hissed, his blue eyes so fierce that Scarlet was shocked into obeying. Liall said several words to the crew again, then took hold of Scarlet's shoulder and began to hurry him toward the cabin.

"Come with me," Liall said icily. "I vouched for your conduct on board and I've just had to explain myself to that swine you hit."

Scarlet wrenched away from Liall's grasp. "I didn't do anything! I was just standing there and he came up and—"

"I understood you the first time." Liall pushed him through the open door of the cabin. "What you do not appear to understand is that you travel on this ship purely on sufferance and I have made my word of honor your bond. You must be more mindful with it."

Scarlet just breathed, so angry that he did not trust himself to answer right away. "Your honor," he said flatly. "Am I supposed to protect yours and forget mine?"

Liall's expression softened. "No, of course not. But with your looks, surely you have dealt with this sort of thing before."

"You have a short memory, Wolf."

Liall looked immediately regretful and reached out to put a hand on Scarlet's shoulder.

"Keep your hands off me," Scarlet said deliberately. Liall's hand halted in mid-air and his expression went blank and emotionless. He turned on his heel so suddenly that the hem of his black cloak snapped behind him, and he left the cabin, closing the door firmly.

In the sudden silence, Scarlet sat on the floor and began going through his pack. If he could not go out, he might at least find something useful to do inside, and some of his clothes needed mending. His mind remained unsettled as he tried to work, and he began to wonder what he had gotten himself into by choosing to follow Liall. What did he know of the man, anyway? Only what Liall had told him and what he had personally observed from Liall's actions, which was a knot of contradictions so tangled that he despaired of unraveling it.

An hour passed before Liall returned. He entered with an apologetic look on his face and sat down on the floor next to Scarlet, his long legs sticking out.

"We both have sharp tempers," Liall said carefully. "So, let us begin again. You must be careful how you behave, Scarlet. I do not want you to see you hurt, yet I cannot protect you from every man on board. That does not mean I would not try, but even I cannot prevail against so many."

Scarlet nodded grudgingly, not looking at him. "All right."

Liall tilted his head, trying to catch Scarlet's eye. "Do you understand? I do not think you were wrong to strike him, but you would have been wiser not to, considering our situation."

"Yes," he sighed.

Liall patted Scarlet's knee, and then withdrew his hand quickly. "I know it is not pleasant, but it is necessity. You must realize that we are, in effect, in my lands now, and you must listen to me and heed my advice."

"I know." Then, because he knew that he would have died if Liall had not nursed him during his fever, Scarlet ducked his head in apology. "I don't mean to be ungrateful."

Liall made a rude noise. "I do not want your gratitude.

It is a meager substitute for friendship." Scarlet remained silent. Liall turned and cupped Scarlet's face in his hands.

"Look at me, pedlar. Your thrice-damned honesty is one of the things I admire most about you. Another is that you do not coldly calculate before you act, but follow your instincts, however foolish they may be. That is honesty, too, in a way. A man always knows where he stands with you, red-coat. I value that." His thumb brushed Scarlet's cheek. "Now that you know how impressed I am with your nature, please... would you try not to be yourself so much, at least for now? It is the only way either of us will reach Rshan."

Scarlet nodded in reluctant assent, mollified by Liall's words even as he detested what was being asked of him. It galled him that to be so out of his element. Liall knew these mariners and their language and their ways. Scarlet had no choice but to rely on him.

Liall released him. The timbers creaked and the silence of the sea closed back in, making Scarlet feel like a creature trapped in a cage.

It would be a mistake to care too much for this boy, Liall chided himself. He had left Scarlet brooding in the cabin and joined Qixa's table for dinner, as the captain had requested. He drew wet rings on the scarred oak table with the moisture beading up and pooling down from his metal wine cup and gave each ring a name. The first was Foolish, the second Reckless. His index finger hovered over the table just before closing the ring, and he named the third one Wrong.

Scarlet was a fraction of his age. Not only that, but Scarlet had never had a lover before. That thought was both attractive and terrifying, for if he fell in love with the pedlar, it would be an attachment not easily broken for either of them. He recalled how unexpectedly difficult he had found it to leave Scarlet for the first time in Byzantur, and then again for the second. Now, the thought of losing Scarlet filled him with a cold dread that he feared had less to do with love than self-preservation. On the day he left Rshan so many years ago, he had vowed to himself that no one, man or woman, would ever find a place in his heart again. The events that led up to that vow had not only shattered his faith in himself and his will to live, but it had very nearly split the kingdom of Rshan asunder.

I do not deserve to love, he concluded, and then was disgusted with himself for entertaining such a mawkish opinion. Impatiently, Liall passed his hand over the table, erasing the marks, and forcibly turned his attention to his host.

Liall knew little of Captain Qixa, but already he was beginning to trust the man. Liall liked his bluff manner, bordering on rudeness, and he observed that Qixa's crew obeyed him swiftly but without fear. This was a captain well-liked by his crew.

The common galley was ripe with the smell of the bilge and the air too close and warm. Liall had not been seasick in decades, but that night was the first time he came close to it since he was a boy. Dining at the captain's table of a brigantine ship and dining among the crew was not too terribly different. The crew ate waybread and salted meat and fresh fish and onions. As far as Liall could see, that was identical to what the captain and his quartermaster and first mate dined on. The only difference was the wine: pale green anguisange wine for their table, ale and imbuo for the crew. It was decent vintage too. Liall told Qixa as much while seated at his right hand. Qixa had tried to give sway and vacate the captain's chair, the place of honor, to Liall, but Liall had been able, with a stern look and a small shake of his head, to dissuade Qixa. There were those on board who knew of his true identity, but he feared pushing his luck too far. The bounty-price to prevent him from ever reaching the shores of Rshan would naturally be very high, perhaps even high enough to tempt a captain of men to seek another career elsewhere. Nemerl was a very large world.

At the lower table, Oleksei, who had been shadowing Liall's steps since he came aboard, raised his wooden cup to Liall in a small toast and grinned, displaying white teeth and comely, curved lips. Liall returned the gesture if not the expression, and was discomfited at the flash of pleasure on Oleksei's face. He wondered what the young man thought of Scarlet. Though it was true that he had led the crew to think of Scarlet as his property, the crew also patently believed them to be lovers. He had not bothered to deny it, feeling that there might be some safety in the fiction for Scarlet. At least it would – or should – render him untouchable by the crew, who might not even see him as human: a pet, perhaps, or just a possession of his that they need not consider beyond that.

Mautan leaned across the table and refilled Liall's cup. "He is better, the lenilyn?" he asked without real interest.

Lenilyn. Outlander. Non-person. "Much better. I thank you," Liall answered tartly. The healer had been next to useless and had not seemed to care if Scarlet lived or died.

The mate grinned and shrugged and scratched under his arm. "Only my job. I was sure the little thing would die. Hilurin, is he? Must be made of tougher stuff than he looks."

"He is," he said, casting a look at Oleksei, whose eyes seemed to be stuck on him.

"I don't see why you bother, myself. I would have pitched the scrawny git overboard just to stop him puking on me."

Liall took a drink of the excellent wine. "That would not do at all."

Qixa chuckled into his mug of wine. "Is he good between the sheets, your outlander?"

Liall realized he had gotten himself into a trap. If he said no, the crew would be even more curious, which might cause more trouble later. As it was, the crew seemed to be settling into the notion that Scarlet was Liall's personal property, and must be tolerated to some extent. Discouraging that view might be disastrous. "He is... inventive," he improvised, which was not a lie.

Mautan made an obscene gesture with his hand that invoked catcalls from the lower table. "I'll bet he's a tight piece, too. Where'd you find him?"

Liall was reluctant to relate the tale of the red-hooded pedlar and the wolf. For some reason, he wanted to keep it to himself, like it was a private moment between them, when it had been nothing of the sort.

Qixa put his mug down with a grave air and placed a sympathetic hand on Liall's shoulder. "Tell me, were you his first? Did you break him in well? Poor lad, to go all your life looking at little Byzan twigs, then to tackle a Rshan oak!"

"We were suitably impressed with each other."

Qixa laughed uproariously and pounded the table until he and Mautan had tears running from their eyes. Mautan was a humorous fellow who often laughed. He and Qixa had a comfortable relationship that reminded Liall of Peysho and Kio, and Liall was suddenly and unexpectedly struck with a pang of longing for his adopted home. Of all the strange things he had known in life, to be suddenly homesick for the Southern Continent, a country he had been raised to think of as barbaric and dirty, peopled with backward savages, took him utterly by surprise. He took a drink to cover it, and his eyes wandered the hall. Below him, he saw that Oleksei was giving Qixa a sour look for having mentioned Scarlet at all.

Liall sighed and looked away before Oleksei could flash his handsome smile again. There were other matters that begged his attention. Liall turned to Qixa and began to ask him, in carefully respectful tones, what he knew of the current situation in Rshan.

Qixa had gossip but no real news of the court, and it was that which Liall needed to hear. The captain knew that the old king-consort was dead, and that the crown prince, whose name was Cestimir, was too young to inherit and could not hold the support of the barons. Scant enough information, and the rest was rumor and fish-wife gossip, useless and probably years old. The food was tasteless and Liall was tired and wanted to lie down, but he could not quit the table until the captain did. Some traditions are courtesy everywhere. The good wine kept him occupied and he refilled his cup again and again, drinking until his headache went away and the stench of the bilge did not bother him so much.

As the night wore on, Scarlet dozed and woke fitfully. He got up several times to drink water and chew on the generous portions of hard waybread and smoked fish Liall had left for his dinner. Though he knew his acute hunger stemmed from his recent sickness and his body's attempt to recoup the weight he had lost, he found it difficult to work up an appetite for the taste of stale waybread and fish. Liall had also left the rose-scented che. He contemplated venturing out for hot water, and then thought better of it. If there was trouble, he would be blamed for it because he disobeyed Liall's orders. That unfairness nettled him, and he settled uncomfortably in the bunk and tried to give his mind some occupation by going over the pedlar's routes to Rusa from Nantua and Dorogi. They were much trickier than the straight routes down the Snakepath through the Nerit and the Bledlands. He had planned, once upon a time, to hire a map-maker to sit down with him and illustrate the circuitous pathways, with their names and hazards and what a pedlar could expect to find on the way, but he supposed that was idle thought now. He had little use for a map of Byzantur at present.

For fun and because there was no one there to see or scold him, he kindled a withy-light in his hand and idly made it weave a dance in and out between the fingers of his left hand, the tiny blue flames very cool against his skin. He was surprised he could make the withy last as long as he did, far longer than he had ever done before. Perhaps his Gift was growing stronger, though he had never heard of anyone's Gift suddenly getting better at his age.

The coals in the small brazier were turning dead gray and Scarlet was thinking about getting up and stoking it when Liall finally returned. The Northman smelled of wine at ten paces and was unsteady on his feet.

"Scarlet!" Liall exclaimed happily, and flung himself down on the bunk next to Scarlet, on the inside near the wall.

Scarlet did not mind that, except that Liall chose next to nuzzle his ear with a wet tongue. For an instant, Scarlet was incredulous, and then, as Liall began to shift over him, he was alarmed. He rolled quickly to one side fell off the bunk, banging his knee.

"You're drunk," he accused.

Liall smiled lazily. "Perhaps a very little, yes."

Scarlet knew too well how it could be when men drank. There were many tabernas in the Ankar souk. "I told you not to touch me," he reminded Liall. "Whatever the crew thinks, I'm not your whore."

Liall sat up. "Have I ever called you that?"

He rubbed his sore knee. "Throwing yourself on me makes me wonder."

Liall looked down the length of his aristocratic nose, and his voice had the quelling tone of a man speaking to an inferior. "You are certainly behaving childishly at the moment."

"Because I don't care to have a drunken man paw at me?"

"Paw at you." Both his white eyebrows arched. "I'm gratified to know precisely how you feel, Scarlet. Pray enlighten me further."

Scarlet wondered if all Liall's words got longer when he drank. "You've been treating me like a child since we boarded this ship and I saved your life in Volkovoi."

Liall examined a loose thread on his cuff. "I was briefly distracted in Volkovoi."

"You were getting your skull beat in."

Liall narrowed his eyes. "I will not linger and quarrel with a child," he said haughtily, and rose unsteadily from the bunk. "Perhaps in the morning you will be clearer-headed."

"One of us will be," he snarled.

Liall ignored this and stalked out with less than his usual grace. The door snapped shut behind him. Scarlet stayed on the floor and dragged some of the blankets off the bunk with him. If Liall stumbled back in, let him wonder why he avoided the bed.

All he did was argue with this man. He was not even sure how he felt about Liall, and here he was, following the man across half the world.

And you want him, he concluded with a sigh, closing his eyes and snuggling deeper in the blankets. The boards of the floor were hard against his back. You want him, but damned if you'll let him know it.

Though he knew it was unfair, Scarlet also realized he still blamed Liall for all the bad things that had happened since they met, as if Liall were the bird-messenger of Deva and had brought ruin riding on his wings. He did not understand the impulse that had prompted him to make that harrowing leap from the dock, but Liall could not be blamed for the fact that Scarlet was not resting at Shansi's house with Annaya, eating spicy persa stew and talking to people in his own language. He could never go back to Annaya.

At least, he thought blackly, not until there was a new Flower Prince in the palace, and perhaps he could explain what Cadan and his soldiers had planned to do to him on that long and deserted stretch of road. He had still not confided everything to Liall.

The dawn came in gray and blustery, bringing a brisk wind that smelled of ice and felt like being buried in snow. Scarlet awoke stiff and freezing. He had slept – what time he had slept? – on the thick pallet with the hard boards pressing his shoulder into numbness. Only a full bladder forced him out into the cold. When he returned, his skin was all goose-flesh and he noted with some astonishment that he could see his breath in the cabin. It was getting measurably colder every day they sailed north.

He was on his knees rolling the pallet up when Liall came in. He looked vaguely unwell.

"Scarlet," he began, and sank down on the bunk with a groan.

"Yes?"

Scarlet heard him sigh. "I crave your pardon for my behavior last night. I'd had more wine than was wise."

Scarlet began sorting through his pack, rearranging it.

"Scarlet."

"Yes, I heard you. You were drunk. And?"

"And I know you are not a whore. Despite our bad beginning, I never intended to treat you like one. Now, will you for the sake of all the gods turn around and come here and not make me shout?"

Scarlet turned and sat on the cold floor, resting his back on the bulkhead. Liall was holding his forehead as if it pained him.

"I was feeling enthusiastic about your presence last night. I intended no insult or—" he groped for the correct word. "Impropriety."

Scarlet said nothing as he regarded Liall, pulling his legs up and dangling one wrist over his knee.

"You really are a right little bastard," Liall said conversationally. "I'm suffering here."

"And I haven't?" Scarlet echoed. His voice turned strident as his temper wore thin, made worse by the cold and his own feeling of isolation, which was beginning to become constant. "I've been ill, I've been propositioned, I spent four days walking the soles of my boots thin, had to fight off murderous thieves on my crossing of the Channel—"

"What?" Liall roared and then held his head.

"—I've been sneered at and mocked and I'm sick to Deva's hells of being cooped up in this stinking cabin!"

"Stinking or not," Liall muttered "you'll stay in it."

"That sounds like an order."

Liall continued to rub his forehead. "Take it for what you will. You may be curious about the crew but they are not, beyond the basest of inquiries, curious about you."

Scarlet gritted his teeth and banged the back of his head lightly against the bulkhead. "I don't even know why I'm here," he grumbled to the ceiling.

"You are here because you've made yourself a wanted man in three countries by killing a Byzan army captain," Liall said deliberately. "Now… who tried to murder you?" He demanded too loudly and closed his eyes again, groaning.

Scarlet waved a hand. "It's not important."

"The hell—" Liall started out loudly and got quieter, "The hell it isn't."

"Let me understand you. It's all right for men to grope me or pay me to grope them, but killing me is strictly out of bounds."

By now, Liall was holding his head in both hands. "You're killing me," he snarled. "Let me say this before my skull cracks open: I'm sorry things have been difficult for you, but there is little I can do about it."

"Maybe not, but that's no reason to punish me."

Liall gave him a look that was so startled and hurt that Scarlet felt ashamed. "You believe I am punishing you?"

"Why are you going back to Norl Udur?"

"I told you."

"You told me very little. I'm sure there's more."

"As you have guessed, there is," Liall replied uncomfortably. "But I am not attempting to punish you. I cannot tell you certain things because it would be dangerous for you to know them. Have you never heard that ignorance is bliss? In your case, ignorance is protection. There are things I will not know for certain until we arrive in Rshan, and I'd rather not risk you."

"Risk me how?"

Liall sighed and sagged a little. "You insisted on coming," he repeated, avoiding a real answer, and he put his hands down to grip the wooden edge of the bunk. "Do you think I enjoy knowing that stinking mariner tried to buy you? Do you think I enjoy drinking and eating with men who have nothing but contempt for you and would happily kill if I were not here to stop them?" He looked unhappy and glanced away for a moment. "As for my behavior last night, it was an excess of drink, not contempt, and... and I am only a man, after all." He risked a glance at Scarlet. "The wish that prompted me to treat you so badly at the Kasiri camp is still very much in force, I fear."

Scarlet grew still. "What wish is that?"

Liall regarded him in strained silence for a long moment. "The wish of a man who wants very much to be your lover, but does not know how to go about it." After a pause wherein Scarlet was held silent purely by surprise, Liall held his hand out to him. "Come, please, let us mend this quarrel. You must trust that there are things I cannot explain to you yet, and trust in what I feel for you."

There was no 'must' about it, but Scarlet relented at the pain in Liall's voice. He got up and sat stiffly beside Liall on the bunk. "It's hard for me to believe you don't know how to go about something, or anything."

"Believe it."

"Is it..." Scarlet paused, thinking. At first, Liall had done the pursuing. Now he felt like he was the one chasing Liall, and suddenly Liall had absented himself from the equation. "Is it something I've done?"

"No," Liall said quickly. He pressed Scarlet's hand. "But I cannot talk about it yet. Please forgive me."

Scarlet sensed the conversation was hopeless. They seemed doomed to misunderstand each other. He changed the subject. "Have you taken anything for that bad head? Maybe you should lie down."

"If I lie down, I will not get up again for the rest of the day," he said and closed his eyes briefly. "With some breakfast and che inside me, I will feel better. I'm also sorry I left you alone last night. That was a foolish thing, considering the mood of the crew. It won't happen again."

Scarlet shrugged, as if it did not matter, but he suspected Liall's eyes saw more keenly, despite the hangover. He offered to scrounge breakfast, but Liall declined.

"Good penance for my indulgence, and the fewer encounters you have with the crew, the better."

3.

Pursued

Someone pounded on the door at the turn of the watch, around dawn or thereabouts. Scarlet had already risen and was careful not to disturb Liall, sitting on the floor and busying himself with repairing a lace on his boot, which looked to be close to falling apart after nearly a month at sea. Liall had already told Scarlet that he was wasting his time mending, but the pedlar did not listen. He would get much better gear for them both in Rshan, and cover Scarlet's white skin in silk.

The knock sounded again and he cracked one eye open. Scarlet glanced at him and then the door, and he nodded. Scarlet was safe enough with him nearby, or as safe as he could make him. The crew's hatred for the foreigner in their midst was a tangible thing, heavy and onerous to live under, but there was no way around it. Scarlet got up and answered the infernal pounding as Liall's hand crept toward the hilts of the knives he kept forever near.

The hatch opened and Oleksei stood there, eyeing Scarlet in hostile silence. He would not even speak to ask for Liall, and the unnecessary rudeness made Liall sharp when he roused himself and edged Scarlet out of the way.

"What?" Liall growled.

"Captain Qixa wants you."

Liall nodded and dismissed Oleksei with a curt gesture. The mariner went, but not without a last glance at the object of his dislike.

"Is something wrong?"

"I do not know yet. Perhaps."

"Can I go with you?"

"No. Remain here."

Liall threw on a woolen coat and slid his hands into a pair of fur-lined gloves. The weather had turned steadily colder day after day, until now they huddled in the cabin most days, conserving body heat and talking about this or that, playing dice, or inventing word games and riddles to stave off boredom. Scarlet had told him so many tales about his family and of the people of erstwhile Lysia that Liall now believed he had known each and every one of them individually. He was a little surprised that his young companion proved to be such an adept storyteller. When asked, Scarlet would only reply that he inherited the talent from his mother. For Liall's part, he did his best to remember the books he had read in childhood. Those were the tales he told, more charming and neat than Scarlet's stories of Lysia, but infinitely less frank. When he ran out of books, he told Scarlet of his years with the Kasiri tribes, and the splendor of the kingdom of Minh, the exotic provinces of Khet, and of the Wasted Lands that lay far to the west, beyond the reach of all civilization. He was sure Scarlet did not believe most of it, especially the tales about Minh, which were stranger than fiction, yet he enjoyed them immensely.

"It sounds very odd," Scarlet would say for the tenth time. And then, once: "My brother Gerda is in Minh, among all those splendors and strange wonders. I wonder if he'd think me as odd as I'd think him?"

In moments of boredom, Liall would consider ruefully that they could have been entertaining themselves in other ways, more pleasurable and heady ones, but that open door led to a dozen others, each thornier and harder to breach than the last, so he let it be. It was enough for now that they had found some middle ground with each other. There were certain compensations: when they bedded down at night in the single cabin bunk, Scarlet lay close to Liall and sometimes accidentally pillowed his head on Liall's shoulder after falling asleep. Liall might have sought to relieve his body then, seeking to quench the fires Scarlet ignited in his bones with the press of his body and the warmth and nearness of his skin, but he dared not. There were too many secrets between them, and Liall had not taken a lover – a real lover – in a very long time. His last experience with love had been catastrophic, to put it mildly.

Liall patted Scarlet's shoulder. "Leave the door open if you wish. They won't trouble you."

"I might trouble them," Scarlet shot back.

Qixa was on the quarterdeck, his breath steaming in the frigid gray dawn. He did not need to ask Qixa what he wanted. The schooner was on the leeward side in the near distance, still far enough away yet, but she was faster than the larger, heavily-laden brigantine and her gaff sails were trimmed for speed. Obviously, she was trying to catch the brigantine. Liall observed the red and yellow flag she flew at high mast.

"Arbyss colors," Qixa said, not believing it a bit. Neither did Liall. "Not at full sail this far north. What are they hurrying to, an iceberg?" There was no trade in the winter with Rshan, and that was the only land that lay on this course. Besides, the schooner moved too swiftly even for full sail. Her holds were empty. Liall surveyed her lines. "No cannon," he stated. "It could be worse."

Liall knew they were in deep trouble. So, apparently, did Qixa. The captain turned and barked orders at Oleksei: secure belowdecks, douse all fires, break out the weapons. Qixa gave Liall a look that spoke much.

"Not my doing, ap kyning. You can believe it."

"I do. This is Faal's work coming home to roost, I suspect. That schooner is not after our cargo."

There was no other sense in the schooner's pursuit: she could not carry away a fifth of their holds, laden with wood and oil and spice and furs, and there was better piracy in warmer waters without the hazards of ice and wind and a well-armed crew of giant Northmen. The Rshani brigantine was altogether too much trouble for mere pirates. No, the cargo they wanted was roughly man-sized and white-haired. Liall did not know for certain who wanted to prevent him from reaching Rshan, but he had a good idea. Now, he resolutely turned his thoughts away from Rshan and to the present. There was to be a battle. Once more, he fiercely regretted last night's wine.

Liall returned to the cabin and found Scarlet seated on the floor mending his boot. Scarlet looked at Liall's face and rose immediately.

"What? What's wrong?"

Liall put his hands on Scarlet's shoulders. "Now, you must listen to me, and do as I say. In a while, perhaps less than an hour, you will hear some noise from topside. I want you to bolt the door and be quiet." Scarlet's own Morturii knives were on the bunk. Liall took one up and slid it from its sheath, putting the hilt in Scarlet's hand. "If anyone tries to force their way in, kill them."

Scarlet looked at the edge of the dark, eerily beautiful knife and then at him. "What's happening?"

"What always happens with men like me. You would have been safer going into the Wasted Lands than following me, little one."

Scarlet seized his arm when Liall would have left quickly. Liall could not look at Scarlet. He was too sick at the thought of what would happen to the pedlar if the crew were not strong enough, if they did not prevail and drive their pursuers back or burn them into the cold sea. He could see the scenario unfolding in his mind's eye: the crew dead, himself fallen or taken, and the bloody raiders finally discovering the bolted cabin and its lone inhabitant.

Beauty, like gold, is coveted everywhere, and being male had never guaranteed Scarlet's safety from certain kinds of assault. There would be the inevitable joking and leers. They would take their time, no longer being in haste, and they would have him as they willed. Liall quailed to think of it, he who had seen so much of blood and death, but the thought of what they would do to Scarlet's flesh made him weak.

It was then, after months of denial, that Liall began to realize he no longer had a choice in whether or not he loved Scarlet. Fear welled up in his chest and he pushed it back savagely. He had loved once and men had died for it. Many futures had been lost, his own among them. He would not make the same mistake again only to watch his world fall apart. Yet, at that moment, he could not imagine any future at all that lay beyond Scarlet's death. The world seemed to drop off at that point; a far vista abruptly severed into a hopeless void.

Liall made to go, keeping the words he wanted to say behind his teeth.

"No," Scarlet urged, stepping after him. "Stay here."

"It's a small difference, but I can be of more use above."

"Then I'm coming with you."

"No!" Liall turned and grabbed Scarlet's shoulders, shaking him hard. "You'll do as I say!"

Scarlet gaped at him, shocked by his sudden violence, and Liall's anger vanished. "I crave your pardon," Liall said in shame.

"I'm not afraid, Liall."

"No. I am the coward here, not you, too weak to watch your blood being spilled." With that, he had no more words to share. Liall shook his head helplessly and released him.

Liall rejoined Qixa on the quarterdeck. Oleksei, Mautan the mate, and the quartermaster were gathered in a knot. For once, Mautan was not smiling, and he looked leeward and saw the schooner had gained greatly just in the time he was gone.

"Keep her on the leeward," he warned. "That will give us some advantage, but not much."

Qixa nodded, his arms crossed, watching the deadly lines of the ship closing on their stern like a sleek hound on the water. There was nothing else he could do.

When she was two hundred paces out, the mate gave a shout to the men on the main deck, all lined up as they were with their knives and swords and hatchets in their hands, silent as the tomb, watching the schooner grow and fill the horizon. At a signal from Qixa, they moved, some shinnying up the ropes and some bellying up to the port-side rail with shields in their hands to deflect arrows. These would try to protect the sails and masts and also hack through any grappling implements thrown at them from the schooner deck.

Liall saw a man marking his forehead with an ancient sign, and another, a mariner with ruddy-gold hair and a face even younger than Oleksei's, looked to the north, toward Rshan, and nodded as if making some silent pact. Watching them was the worst part; the knowing. Watching them slip up behind and then alongside bit by bit and seeing their numbers, the weapons in the hands of the enemy crew, their set faces. There were a lot of them. Not Rshan, thank Deva, but lean, brown-haired Morturiis and stout, parchment-skinned axe men from Minh. He had been wrong about the empty holds; they were filled with fighters.

It did not take long. The Ostre Sul dove into a thick fog that seemed to have rolled in from nowhere, smelling of fish and rot, and clouding their vision. The brigantine's sails vanished into white clouds.

They raced now, neck and neck into the north, and when the length of water between them was perhaps fifty paces, the schooner captain gave a shout. Some of the enemy crew leaped forward to the rail then, succumbing to nerves or just tired of standing. The captain, a grizzled Morturii commander in blackened Minh armor who straddled the quarterdeck as if bolted there, signaled for the hooks.

The grappling hooks, iron claws attached with strong rope at one end, were thrown. Some missed the brigantine and trawled the sea uselessly; others struck the gunwale and held fast, their strong barbs sunken deep into wood or jammed between crevices. The Rshani crew leaped to hack the ropes that held them, and the Morturii captain shouted another order. Arrows flew from the schooner. One volley – all there would be time for before their two hulls began to scrape – and several of the men nearest the railing screamed and fell, impaled through the chest and arms.

The compact size of the Minh warriors gave them an advantage. From the schooner, the Minh were shinnying or swinging over on the grappling ropes, either to prevent the hooks from being dislodged or to drop like spiders on the Rshani crew from above.

Liall had put aside his knives and taken a sword from the weapons master. He had had it in his hand from the moment the arrows flew. It was a long, double-edged blade, probably Qixa's own, and felt good in his grip. They – the watchers higher up on the quarterdeck, Liall,

Qixa, the quartermaster and Mautan, Oleksei and perhaps thirty other skilled fighters – waited for the arrows to land before they moved a muscle. One volley of arrows was all Liall expected, since they were at such close quarters.

He was not wrong, and as the Minh archers dropped their bows to the deck and blades flashed from their sheaths, Liall charged off the foredeck with Mautan and the others, roaring loud enough to wake the dead. Half of all soldiery is intimidation, and he made best advantage of his height and appearance. A Morturii swordsman rose in his path and he struck the man down as he passed, fixed on a target near the port anchor; a hook embedded in a post. Two of the fighter's fellows tried to take him down and he turned to slaughter them, wielding the double-edged sword like an axe, felling them like saplings.

Liall struck down another Minh on his way to the side, sword straight into him and out, not even stopping to make sure he was dead. Then a larger Morturii blocked his way and they fought briefly. The Morturii was enthusiastic with his weapon, but no true swordsman. At the last, he gave up parrying Liall's thrusts and maneuvers and simply threw himself at the taller man. Liall went down with him and the Morturii rolled and kicked, seeking to get his hands around Liall's throat, but Liall snatched up a dislodged hook in the deck and pushed the barbs into the Morturii's face.

Dazed but on his feet again, Liall hacked at a hook stuck firm in the brigantine's side and cut it away as an enemy crashed over him again and dragged him into the thick of the killing, rolling and tumbling.

Again, Liall threw them off and rose, and while he was fighting his way back to the side to detach more hooks, another Morturii clothed in flamboyant armor and armed with a long-knife in each hand came at him. The Morturii was good. Liall lurched aside from one well-aimed thrust, but the Morturii's left blade went shallowly into his shoulder. The man took a fool's moment to grin at his handiwork and Liall smashed a fist into the Morturii's jaw and watched his smirking head snap back. Liall used his knife to open a wide, red smile in the man's throat.

On the schooner, the Minh were hauling on the ropes, dragging the tethered schooner close to their side, at last sealing their wet hulls, which screeched like mating wildcats. They lashed the ropes to their ship to make them fast, and then began to leap the distance between them, three at a time. Soon, enemy fighters swarmed over the Ostre Sul's deck.

The Rshani crew were in grave trouble. They were outnumbered two to one, and they had already lost many to the arrows. They had only one hope: to cut the ropes that bound the ships together and swing away from the schooner into the swell, separating the raiders on their deck from the greater numbers of their fellows on the schooner. Then they could kill the enemies that remained on their ship and then face the second wave.

Liall found another hook and chopped the rope free with his sword, then instinctively dropped to one knee when he heard a whirring at his back. The axe that narrowly missed his ear smashed into wood, and he stabbed back with his knife without looking, and the gut-stabbed mariner tumbled over him. Liall helped him into the sea while keeping a firm grip on his knife. Losing a blade stuck in another man's throat or kidney had killed more mariners over the years than scurvy.

It was close and dirty fighting from that point: stabbing up under the ribs, wielding the sword crudely, chop and hack and slash as the battle became more like butchery than war. He went down once under a press of Morturii and took the opportunity to hamstring two or three of them, then rose from the deck, throwing the bodies off him with a roar. A Minh swordsman darted in under his guard and thrust upwards. Liall danced aside, but not swiftly enough, and the enemy blade pierced his shoulder where the Morturii had stabbed him already, deep but not lethal. If he had not turned, the Minh would have taken him down and impaled him to the wooden deck.

Fresh blood can steam like hot water in the north, and new blood poured out of him in a misty fount, hot and smelling of slaughter. Howling, Liall hacked at the Minh swordsman until he had lopped off an arm, then kept going from there. The Minh was considerably abbreviated when he was done.

When Liall blinked away the haze before his eyes, he saw that Scarlet had disobeyed him and joined the battle. He was near the bulkhead that supports the quarterdeck, fighting a spear-wielding Morturii a head taller than him, and as he watched, Scarlet slashed with his long-knife – too slow! – and narrowly avoided being spitted.

Liall went a little mad as the berserker rage took over, but this time he welcomed it. He only knew there was a roar in his ears like the sea and his throat hurt from screaming, and all around him was steaming blood and the stink of fear and men falling like wheat under his blade. He saw Scarlet twice more: once hacking away at a grappling rope while a hulking Minh ran at him. Scarlet fell back and grabbed the nearest thing, a broken spar with a jagged end, pointed it at his enemy, and let momentum do the rest for him. Liall tried to fight his way to Scarlet's side, but Scarlet had already moved closer to the half deck, where the fighting was less, having achieved his goal and dislodged the rope. The second time, Liall saw him locking blades with a Minh who was a much better swordsmen. The Minh slapped the blade out of Scarlet's grip with his sword, slicing the back of his hand, and Scarlet danced back a step and looked wildly around for another weapon. Liall threw his dagger at the Minh and caught him where his spine joined his neck. The Minh fell to the deck, his feet jerking as he convulsed and frothed like a rabid dog. Scarlet stared at Liall, dazed and pale.

"Get below!" Liall roared.

The Minh fell before Scarlet with Liall's dagger in his neck, and Scarlet fell back against the ship, pressing his body against the reassuring strength of solid wood. The deck felt slick beneath his feet, and he looked down and saw that his boots were washed with blood. Everywhere he looked he saw visions of madness. Men hacked into each other, their faces twisted into unrecognizable masks of straining fury, as blood sprayed from the wounds of their enemies, bathing all in crimson. He ran.

Suddenly, another Minh warrior loomed before him. The Minh's dark armor blackened the sky, seeming to shut out hope. *On Deva danaee shani,* Scarlet prayed automatically. He had no more weapons, and the bodies of the dead blocked his escape from all sides. Scarlet knew that he looked on his death.

The Minh raised his axe. *Liall,* Scarlet thought in profound loss, and then the Minh opened his wide, bearded jaw, and a torrent of blood flowed from it like a red stream.

Scarlet gaped as the Minh fell, revealing Qixa's broad figure standing behind the fallen warrior. The captain locked eyes with Scarlet and shook his head, a small smile on his lips, as if ridiculing himself for the act of saving a worthless lenilyn.

"Get off the deck, Byzan child," Qixa growled.

Scarlet's whole body was shaking as he nodded at Qixa, unable even to summon a word of thanks. Qixa turned and barked orders to the crew, and for the moment the battle moved away from them both, giving Scarlet a much-needed moment to breathe. He spied a long-knife on the deck and took it up, and then looked out over the water to the enemy schooner.

The Rshani crew had cut away the last of the grappling ropes, and the schooner lurched away from the brigantine. Even Scarlet, novice that he was, could see that it was only a temporary respite. The schooner was faster and could turn much quicker than the brigantine. She could stalk them for weeks on the water, attacking at any moment of her choosing, picking a little more of the Rshani crew off each time, until there were not enough mariners to beat the enemy crew back, or until the winds failed the Ostre Sul and she became a sitting target.

Scarlet's eyes fastened on the billowing sails of the schooner, and he suddenly wished he had Scaja's talent of farcasting his Gift. Scaja had spent many nights teaching his son how to cast the withy on something outside of the house that neither of them could see, a piece of wood in the lane, or a fish deep in the pond. Scarlet had always been able to use his Gift on objects or creatures within arm's reach, but to cast across distance required special skill. A fire on the schooner would solve many things, and if the wind was in their favor, might even do the job for them.

Scarlet knew it was useless, and the schooner was pulling further away with every second. Yet, even as he thought of setting a withy to the enemy sails, he felt a tingling in his skin, like a ripple through his veins, and a flush of heat flooding his face. *I can do it*, he thought.

He had never tried with anything this far away before,

but that fact seemed irrelevant. He stared at the sails, his eyes very wide, and thought: *fire.*

A curl of smoke huffed from the edge of a white sail. Scarlet trembled, for he now felt like he was holding a wild beast by the neck. Flames licked the sail and sent testing fingers to the wood of the schooner's mast. Power surged through Scarlet's body, stirring his blood, hammering his heart, and he recoiled in horror as he felt a man's clothing catch fire on the schooner.

A shout went up among the Rshani as one of the schooner's mainsails was engulfed in flames, and Scarlet jumped, startled, as Qixa bellowed at his men, giving an order Scarlet could not translate. The ten Rshani archers in reserve on the quarterdeck opened fire, felling the enemy fighters who had dropped their weapons and were attempting to put out the fire on their decks.

Qixa gave another order, and the archers launched two volleys of oil-soaked arrows. Twenty trails of flame went up.

Scarlet knew almost nothing of seafaring, yet he instinctively understood that all mariners must have a terror of fire at sea. One look at the blood-soaked deck of the brigantine told him that the Rshani crew could not withstand another assault. There was no other way.

A sail rigging caught fire on the schooner and then another at the aft, and then a great many of the schooner crew began to ignore the battle to fight the more pressing war on their own deck. The wind chose to shift at that moment, fanning the flames and dragging the brigantine safely away. Scarlet lost sight of the schooner in the fog.

No doubt they fought it bravely, but not much later, when the screams floated ghostlike over the misty swells, Scarlet knew the schooner crew had lost their battle with fire. In the new quiet, he grabbed the rail in both hands and leaned over, breathing in great gulps of cold air and trying not to vomit. His mind was like a fly caught in a web, tearing and flailing at itself to escape. What's happening? he thought in dismay. How did I do that? Not even Scaja could have sent a withy like that, and I sent not one, but many, and much stronger than anything I've ever seen Scaja do! What's happening to me?

Behind him, Qixa moved among the crew and ship, surveying the damage. The masts were whole and only one sail was damaged, but all the ship's rails was seriously marred and weakened, as well as the deck on the port side. They would have to drop men over the side on ropes to inspect the hull and determine whether the impact from the schooner bellying up to them had pushed in the wooden hull below the waterline. As for the dead, Scarlet counted eighteen Rshani, among them Mautan the mate, who would never smile again. He did not see Liall anywhere, and fear clutched his heart.

The mariners were dumping the pirate dead overboard when Scarlet finally spotted Liall on the main deck, near the stern. Liall had a sword sheathed at his waist and he held a bloodied hand to his shoulder. He was shouting hoarsely.

"Scarlet!"

"Here!" Scarlet called. He watched, dazed, as Liall came toward him in a rush. Liall seized his shoulders.

"I told you to stay below!" Liall shouted, and then jerked Scarlet this way and that to see if he was whole. "Are you hurt?" he demanded.

Dark blood was spattered at Liall's shoulder and painted down the front of his coat. "No, but you are."

Liall was breathing heavily. "It is nothing."

Scarlet yanked Liall's coat open and flinched when he saw how much blood was soaked into the gray wool of Liall's shirt. "You said there was a curae on board?"

Liall waved that aside, seeming unconcerned. Blood

began dripping in a steady trickle from the end of Liall's shirt, spattering the crimson-washed deck. "I am not the only man wounded on this ship, and there is still work to be done."

"And you'll be no help to anyone if you faint."

Liall scanned Scarlet's body up and down. "Is any of that blood your own?"

Scarlet looked down at his clothes and felt briefly giddy, seeing all the gore. He looked worse than Liall did. "No." His stomach turned over and he was mortally glad he had not eaten for hours. "Never mind me. I have to look at that wound."

"The bleeding has stopped, mostly," Liall said as a last protest.

Scarlet thought Liall looked pale, considering his usual color, and without asking he shoved his shoulder under Liall's arm and steered the man toward their cabin.

Captain Qixa stopped them on the way and spoke to Liall. Liall locked eyes with the captain and gave him a look of deep regret. "This is my fault," Liall said in Bizye. "You know what they were really after."

Qixa shook his head, his face proud but haggard with loss. "No one makes me do anything, ap kyning. I knew the risk."

Liall bowed his head, equal to equal, and Qixa returned it with the aplomb of a king before barking an order to the crew in Sinha. The mariners began to throw the corpses overboard. All, that is, save the Rshani. Mautan they bore gently away on their shoulders, singing a song of death.

Liall allowed Scarlet to guide him into the cabin, and sat slumped on the bunk as Scarlet hurried to find the small pack of medicines he always carried on the road. Scarlet left to dip a basin of fresh water from the barrel on the main deck and returned to find Liall flopped onto his back.

Frightened, Scarlet leaned over Liall and roughly shook his uninjured shoulder.

Liall opened his eyes blearily. "What?"

"I thought you'd passed out."

"I did." Liall sat up painfully. "This is how I heal."

That explained much, including how easily Liall slipped into sleep at the inn at Volkovoi and how quickly his bruises had vanished afterwards. Scarlet managed to get Liall out of his coat and the shirt off him. The wool shirt was ruined, cut in several places and soaked through with blood. He laid it aside and bit his lip when he saw the wide gash at Liall's shoulder.

"This will need stitching," he said.

Liall assessed Scarlet quietly with that measuring gaze of his, his pale eyes revealing nothing. He nodded. "Help me get my boots off. I am covered in blood."

Scarlet helped Liall to undress before turning to the small brazier. Water would have to be heated, and there were bandages to make. He wished suddenly that Hipola the midwife was here, or even Scaja, who had known much more about healing than he did. He could find no suitable cloth to bind the wound with, but he tore one of his older shirts and boiled it in the water. They would do for cleaning the wound, anyway. With the sterilized cleaning cloths laid aside, he dumped the hot water and refilled the iron pot with clean water to heat, boiling it for several minutes to kill off any lingering poisons.

Scarlet took a deep breath and set to work on Liall's shoulder. Liall shuddered a few times as Scarlet cleaned the wound thoroughly, but otherwise held perfectly still and made no protest, even when Scarlet's fingers dug inside his torn flesh to check for bits of metal or wood lodged in the wound.

The cut had bled profusely. A smaller man, a Hilurin

or Aralyrin, would have been dead already from it. Liall began to shiver as Scarlet wiped the last of the blood away and heaped blankets over him and around him, leaving only the wound bare.

"I'll get the thread," Scarlet said.

"Do you know how to do this?"

Scarlet took a deep breath. "Yes. Scaja showed me. I've done it for horses, but never a man."

"Flesh is flesh. You will do fine."

Scarlet smiled wanly over his shoulder. "I should be the one comforting you, not the other way 'round."

There was a knock at the hatch and Liall snapped to alertness. Scarlet answered it and found a straight-faced mariner with a bundle in his hands. The bundle proved to be clean linen for binding and dressing a wound. Scarlet thanked the man, but the mariner turned on his heel and left, not acknowledging him. It seemed that Byzans were still enemy even after they allied with Rshani in battle.

Scarlet set the bundle near Liall and opened his small packet of medicines to take out the needle and boiled thread. There was some yellow sulfa powder in there, too, fine as dust and smelling faintly of rotten eggs. This he sprinkled painlessly on Liall's wound before he put the needle through the candle flame. It took him three tries to thread the needle. He sat beside Liall.

"You'll need to hold very still," he warned.

"Just do it."

Liall held quiet, aside from an occasional tremor as his muscles tightened. Scarlet forced himself not to think of it as living flesh as he concentrated on making the stitches small and neat. The wound was cleanly- made and the cut had slid deep sideways, rather than in. To Scarlet, it appeared that Liall had spun out of reach before the blade could thrust forward, and the edge had slid over the top of his muscle, creating a long, deep gash that bled much, but had failed to strike any vital areas.

Liall was barely awake when Scarlet cut the last stitch and readied the linen packing for the wound. He wound strips of linen under and around Liall's arm, and then made a small, careful knot.

Scarlet nodded with satisfaction. "That should hold."

"Good job," Liall said faintly. "Now... I will rest for a bit." But he struggled to open his eyes. "I told you to stay below."

Scarlet shrugged.

"I looked for you," Liall said. "At the end, when the battle turned to our favor, I could not see in the mist and the smoke. I was frightened," he admitted.

"You?" Scarlet scoffed. "Never."

"I realized," Liall said slowly "what an opportune moment it was to be rid of an unwanted passenger." He flinched when he saw the shock in Scarlet's eyes. "One well-placed knife in the midst of battle and no one would think it strange."

"I know the crew doesn't care for me," Scarlet said, shaken. "But why would any of them want me dead?"

"I did not say they did. And I do not truly believe that anyone is planning it, but... my experience with the nature of men does not allow me to take risks." He reached for Scarlet's hand and his voice turned softer. "I really did not believe you would stay below. You have too much heart to stay hidden while others fight for their lives."

"Don't bet on it," Scarlet returned tartly. "Now that I've seen a battle, I realize I don't care to see another. Ever. If those pirates come back, you might find me hiding in a barrel." Scarlet belatedly remembered Liall throwing the blade into the Morturii's throat. "Thanks for throwing that knife."

Liall produced a sickly grin and Scarlet pulled the last blanket over him. Scarlet burned the cloth he had used to clean Liall's wound in the brazier, and when he finished this task he saw that Liall was fast asleep. Now he could see to his own injuries, if there were any.

His clothing was beginning to stiffen with blood, so he stripped to the skin in the cold cabin, shivering as he washed himself with the last of water. It was then that he discovered that some of the blood on him was his own, after all. He had a few slashes here and there, nothing that cleaning and salve would not take care of. He washed the cuts carefully with water and pressed the yellow powder over the red lines and forgot about them.

Captain Qixa entered the cabin without knocking just as Scarlet had finished dressing in his only other set of clean clothing. Qixa cast a narrow look at Scarlet as he checked Liall's wound, pursing his lips and nodding in grudging approval.

"Very good," Qixa said in heavily-accented Bizye. "He will sleep now, and wake strong. Watch for fever."

Scarlet nodded. "I'll care for him." It was the first time he had spoken to Qixa since the voyage began.

Qixa stared at Scarlet. "You fought hard, lenilyn child. The odds were very bad, but we won anyway. Perhaps you are not bad luck, after all," Qixa said, and then went out quickly, as if he were afraid Scarlet would take it as a compliment.

Scarlet gave the hatch a sour look and piled their bloodied clothing into a heap. Later, he would see about washing them, but just now the constant, brassy stink was making his head hurt. Liall was snoring softly.

"Sure, leave me all the work, just like at Volkovoi," Scarlet muttered in amusement. "I'd rather be working than hurt, though, so you sleep on, Wolf."

Liall sighed in his sleep. Clean and dry, Scarlet carefully crawled into the bunk beside Liall and closed his eyes as exhaustion claimed him. They could all have died out here in the cold sea, their bodies dumped, the ship stolen, and no one would have known what happened. Annaya would never have waited and wondered until Liall the Wolf faded from memory.

He fell into dreamless sleep, but woke later with a start, his heart leaping in his throat. It was near dark, and he reached over to feel Liall's skin, which was warm and damp to the touch. He pressed the back of his hand to Liall's throat to feel the rapid beat of his pulse, wondering if blood loss caused fever in these strange Rshani or if the wound were becoming inflamed or if he should wake the captain.

But the symptom did not seem strange, given the nature of Liall's injury. He fell back asleep. The next dawn, he was sorry that he had not called for the captain. Liall was sweating and tossing in the bunk, his bronze skin gone gray as ash. Liall slept much, and when he did rouse to partial consciousness, it was only to slap aside the cup of water Scarlet tried to force down his throat or to cry out a name – Nadei! – in a tone so heartbroken that it wrote questions across Scarlet's mind.

Qixa, when he came again, did not seem concerned. He made a see-saw motion with his beefy hand. "It is often so. Wait a day or three."

Or three? Scarlet scowled, but there was little he could do. He stayed with Liall throughout the day, feeding him broth and the delicate, rose-scented che that he whispered a withy chant over, first being careful to check that Liall was sound asleep. Liall never woke fully, and the fever did not want to depart his bones. It would leave him for an hour and then flare back again. At sunset, Scarlet slept beside Liall, one hand on Liall's chest to serve as an alarm should the man stir or thrash out of the bunk. At dawn, Scarlet was woken by Liall trying to get out of the bunk.

Scarlet seized hold of Liall's arm and pulled him back.

"No, you must lie down."

"Scarlet, let me up before I piss myself," Liall growled.

He let go. "Oh, you've been feverish, I thought... never mind."

Liall wrapped a blanket around him and stumbled out of the cabin. When he returned, he lit a candle before seating himself heavily in the chair to survey the wreck Scarlet had made of the cabin. Liall looked years older, sitting there with nothing but a blanket around his waist and the bandages covering his shoulder and chest.

"You stayed with me, cared for me." Liall said, as if this were a puzzle he was trying to solve.

"Did you think I'd pitch you overboard?"

Liall gave Scarlet a weary look and rose. Scarlet moved over to make room as Liall climbed back into the bunk.

"Some would." Liall tried to peer under his bandage.

Scarlet pulled Liall's hand away. "Leave that alone."

Liall clasped Scarlet's hand. He looked at the slender, pale fingers against the dark skin of his palm. It was Scarlet's left hand, the one with only four fingers. "I owe you my thanks."

"It was nothing."

Liall released him. "Then it follows that my life is nothing." He stared stonily at the ceiling. "This is the second time I have reason to be grateful to you. Your debt to me, if it ever was a debt, is paid."

Scarlet rose up on his elbow. "That's not for you to decide."

"Even so," Liall said stubbornly "I consider it paid. We are even now."

Scarlet did not know whether to be amused or annoyed.

"Because you say so?"

"I..." Liall faltered and stopped. He turned his head

to look up at Scarlet. "I do not want you to be grateful to me any longer. I want nothing from you that you do not give willingly, of yourself alone, and not from gratitude or your sense of duty. Do you understand?"

Scarlet thought he might. Steeling himself, he reached over and placed his hand upon the thickened pad of bandages over Liall's wound. "This was close, just above your heart."

To Scarlet's surprise, Liall suddenly shifted away from him and turned his head. "The man was not trying for my heart. He wanted my head, but he was clumsy."

It felt like a rebuke. Scarlet withdrew his hand slowly and rolled over on his back. He watched the sway of the lantern and wondered if he should try again to reach Liall or abandon the effort. Perhaps he had made a mistake. Perhaps Liall had changed his mind about desiring him some time ago.

Liall broke the silence. "You say this was your first real battle?"

"Yes." Then, suspiciously, "Why do you ask?"

"Not just because you are Hilurin," Liall said, divining his thoughts. "Because you are young and you were never trained as a warrior should be, and I know how dealing death can haunt a man."

Scarlet nodded. He could accept being seen as young, but not as weak simply because he was not a ten-foot-tall foreigner with pale hair. "I don't like killing," he said slowly "but I won't be killed without a fight."

"You are a brave man," Liall said softly, and just that quickly, he closed his eyes and was asleep again.

Scarlet felt Liall's skin again and sagged in relief when he found it cool and dry. Shivering dully, he pulled the blankets up to Liall's chin, too weary even to feel the cold before he drifted back into sleep. He woke perhaps an hour later and went out to fill the water skins and fetch fresh bandages from the mate who was on watch, an affable man named Ulero who was Mautan's replacement, and – like Mautan – much less hostile than his fellows. Qixa was nowhere to be seen, and Scarlet remembered that Liall had commented that he and Mautan were close. At least Mautan would be missed by someone.

When Scarlet returned, he was afraid he would wake Liall if he got back into the bunk, so he made another pallet on the floor. When Liall woke later, he cursed Scarlet roundly for freezing himself on the floor. Scarlet was so relieved that Liall felt well enough to be angry, he didn't even argue.

4.

Rough Seas

Liall tried to sleep. The roll and pitch of the ship soothed him, as it always did, but it also deviled his memory. Sleep, fool, he thought with his eyes closed. Some of my best and worst memories are tied up in the sway of a deck beneath me. It was on a ship that I fled from Rshan the first time, an exile, disgraced and aching and tormented by what I had done. I loved sailing as a boy, and Nadei...

He cut the thought short, knowing through long experience that it was unwise to think of that person in the aftermath of a battle. His thoughts would only become darker and fouler until the cage of his brain threatened to drag him down into darkness.

Liall concentrated on breathing, eyes still shut. The timbers of the cabin creaking and the rush of the swell against the hull should have gentled him to sleep, but it did not.

Nadei was eight and Liall was seven, and they were on the water. The air was cold and Nenos was teaching the boys how to row. Liall had shouted at him, laughing: *Nadei! Do not stand up in the boat, you will tip us over!* Nadei was always so certain of himself, so stubborn and reckless. Liall had to watch out for him in a hundred ways, as if he were the elder and not Nadei. They were always together, day and night, sleeping in the same ways, as if he were the elder and not Nadei. They were room, learning from the same teachers, eating from the same plate, brothers in blood and bone.

Liall gritted his teeth and rolled over in the bunk, squeezing his eyes tighter against the smarting tears that threatened. He mentally ticked off the numbers: sixty years and a handful of months since he had last seen Nadei. What had happened to Rshan in that time, to his home, his family? He flung out his arm, expecting to find warmth next to him, and touched a cold, empty space. He opened his eyes and rolled over.

Scarlet was sitting silent in the chair beneath the port hole, wide awake. It was perhaps eight days after the pirate battle.

"You have done that before," Liall said slowly. "Watched me while I slept."

Scarlet blinked lazily and nodded.

The timbers creaked and the thin shadow of a fingernail moon flowed into view through the porthole, just over Scarlet's head. It had waxed and waned three times since they had left Volkovoi. Liall watched the silver sickle drift in and out of the black eye as the ship rode the waves, gazing at him. It was a weightless silence with comfort in it, and words seemed an intrusion.

It was Scarlet who broke the spell. "I like to watch you sleep. You look... more like someone I'd know."

A curious thing to say, but it made sense. Since Scarlet had begun, Liall decided to forge ahead. "There is something between us, is there not? Something more than just my attraction for you and yours for me. Something we haven't spoken of yet."

After a long moment, Scarlet sat forward a little in the chair and folded his hands as if in prayer. "I dreamed about you last night. You were riding a gray horse with a blue banner."

A sharp hurt struck Liall in the center of his breastbone.

"Go on."

"I called out to you, but you wouldn't answer me, and then you left on a ship with great white sails, and I stood on the shore and called to you, but you wouldn't come back." Scarlet rubbed his hands together slowly. "It made me sad. Then I woke up and I was here with you, and after all these months when I thought you wanted me, now you don't seem to. Plus, the crew..." he bit his lip and struggled with the next part of it. "These men look at me in a way I'm unused to. They don't have any respect for me, not because I'm young or because I'm a pedlar, but just because I'm Hilurin and they assume I'm with you because you pay me to be with you, or because you own me like you would own a dog or a horse." He looked down. "It hurts my pride to be thought of as a bought thing."

"Thank you," Liall answered at length "for being so honest with me." He began to get up.

"Whoa," Scarlet quickly rose and pushed him back with the flat of his palm on Liall's chest, his knee on the bunk. "Hold on. You got the truth out of me. I'll have my measure in return, thank you."

"Ah. Of what?"

Scarlet blew his breath out in exasperation and shook his finger in Liall's face. "See here, if you weren't hurt, I'd clout you one for that. I've about had enough of your fancy language and smart ways. Just give me plain talk for once."

Liall raised my hands in surrender and fell back on the bunk, smirking. "Spare me, gentle lord."

"Very funny. Now tell."

His smile faded. There was something too honest in Scarlet's eyes, something that looked too deep into him. It seized any words he had and held them back. "I do hold a... a certain affection for you. You already know this"

"And?"

"And I..."

"Yes?"

"Scarlet, please," Liall averted his eyes, turning his face to the wall. "You cannot know what this is like for me."

"I certainly can't, if you don't tell me."

Damn him. "My heart," Liall began, feeling his throat begin to close up. "Good gods, Scarlet, if you think the seas here are cold, you do not know what my heart was like before I saw you. I have not loved another in a very long time."

Scarlet's mouth twitched into a small, hesitant smile.

"Are you saying—"

Liall pushed himself up and him away, his pulse hammering. Suddenly, the cabin felt small and airless. I am about to suffocate, he thought wildly. "Cease this questioning, can you not?" he snapped, almost gasping.

Scarlet reached out to him. "Liall."

"I will not be badgered!" Liall shouted, and Scarlet recoiled.

"But," Scarlet stammered. "You started this."

Liall was frightened enough of the feelings woken inside him to lash out. "I asked if we were going to be lovers, if we were going to share our bodies. What you are asking me to share is something altogether different."

The words took a moment to sink in, during which time Liall had serious visions about cutting his own tongue out.

Like dousing a candle flame, the warmth went out of Scarlet's young face. "I see." He rose and began putting on his coat, his gaze averted.

"Scarlet."

Scarlet busied himself with his buttons and turned away, ignoring Liall even when he stood and drew near.

"Scarlet, wait."

"I'm going out on the deck to look at the moon," Scarlet told him conversationally, pulling on his gloves.

"If you want to stop me, you'd better hope that your stitches hold, for I'm tired of being told what to do by a man who wants nothing more of me than what's between my legs."

"I lied." Liall grabbed his arm and turned him around. Scarlet hissed in pain and Liall let him go, mindful that he had wounds, too. "I lied, Scarlet. I care about you very much." He took a deep and shaking breath, watching Scarlet. "It costs me greatly to say that, so you can believe me."

Scarlet gazed at Liall with pity. "Who has done this to you, Liall? Who betrayed you so badly that even the thought of love terrifies you?"

He could only shake his head. "I cannot say. I cannot."

Scarlet looked again at the door, as if trying to decide.

"Do not go," Liall asked quietly. Then, more softly, "Forgive me, please."

Scarlet sagged a little and gave a small laugh as he brushed his unkempt hair out of his eyes. "I've been thinking; when we first met, it felt like you were chasing me. I wished you'd stop and just leave me alone. Now I feel like I'm chasing you."

Liall stared at him, then put his hand on Scarlet's chest, just over his heart, and left it there. Scarlet's heart beat with a slow, trusting rhythm, and his warmth seeped into Liall's palm. Liall shook his head sadly.

"Therein is the problem, little Byzan. You have already caught me." Scarlet began to answer him, but Liall put his fingers to Scarlet's mouth. "No more," he begged. "Not just yet. Can we not sit quietly together?"

Scarlet nodded, though Liall saw it was an effort for

him. How this Hilurin hated to let go of an argument! They sat together until the moon drifted under the sea and the colorless dawn slipped in thin and sibilant as a whisper in the dark. Soon, there would be no more dawns, for in less than twenty days they would cross into the Seas of Night and the sun would become a memory.

And he is not ready for it, Liall worried, taking Scarlet's hand. Scarlet allowed it and even slid closer to rest his head on Liall's shoulder.

He is not ready and you are not ready, he mused. And the past will not heal. It draws nearer.

Liall's wound healed well over the next week and was nearly closed when Qixa requested that Liall and Scarlet stay off the main deck as much as possible. Once they crossed into the Nor'Uhn, the great North Sea, there was little to do, and the hazards of ice and heavy winds made it more sensible for the passengers to stay below, Qixa explained.

After the pirate raid, Qixa seemed to think it was his personal responsibility to deliver Liall to Rshan in one piece. It was also true that the closer they came to Rshan, the more likely another attack would be.

So here we are, Liall thought as another long afternoon with Scarlet droned by. Just the two of us penned together in a small space. You would think that would make me happy.

Instead, Liall found he was growing increasingly morose and ill-tempered. He talked no more of love with Scarlet, and after three days the monotony of listening to the sea batten against the hull and the wind whistle through the cracks of the porthole began to weigh heavy on him. He taught Scarlet to speak a little Sinha to pass the hours, teaching him the nuances of certain words, how to say simple greetings and the names of everyday things. Scarlet was a quick study and forgot nothing, and Liall was amazed at his memory. Then, he recalled that a pedlar who could not read or keep books would have need of a sharp memory. Scarlet's pronunciation was so far off that Liall despaired of Scarlet ever making himself understood once they reached Rshan, but the pedlar never gave up trying, even when it was painfully obvious that a lifetime of speaking Bizye had left him unable to curl his tongue around the more complex Sinha consonant blends.

"Hunge sinir ch'th sun rl'er'r."

Liall smiled, which made Scarlet scowl and purse his mouth to try again. It still sounded like toddler speech. If Scarlet spoke to anyone in Rshan with that abominable accent, they would laugh at him.

"Try blowing your breath out a bit more when you say the words, Scarlet. You will never make yourself understood if you do not speak with more strength."

"If I speak with any more strength, I'm going to be spitting."

Liall shrugged. "At least you will be saying good morning when you spit, not 'where is the bear buried'?"

"You just made that up," Scarlet accused.

"Nothing of the sort. Here, try again; *hunge sinir ch'th—*"

When Scarlet tired of learning and Liall wearied of teaching, tedium returned and Liall settled for watching Scarlet as a pastime: the way the candlelight shaded the hollows of his cheeks, the way he combed his black hair in the morning, how softly he slept at night, on his back with his very slender left hand curled on his chest.

After a day or two, when the initial flattery wore off, the attention naturally began to wear thin. Scarlet caught Liall watching him mend a shirt as he sat on the floor under the porthole. It was perhaps the tenth time that day he had seen Liall's eyes fixed on him, and he blew out a short sigh and looked away.

"Liall," he said, then nothing more.

Liall let a minute pass but kept watching. He was enjoying the shape of Scarlet's body, how he so effortlessly reclined on the hard surface, the torn shirt in his lap and one leg folded under him.

"What?" Liall asked easily.

"Would you please stop that?"

"Stop what?"

"Watching me."

Liall was lying on the bunk on the other side of the cabin, his palm resting against his cheek. He sat up and shrugged. "There is nothing else to watch."

"Well, find something," Scarlet snapped. He sighed. "I'm sorry."

"Come over here and kiss me," Liall found himself saying. He was determined to bury his fear and continue on the path he had chosen.

Scarlet looked up quickly, his eyebrows climbing high.

"We can at least kiss, can we not? Or are we to be forever chaste lovers, like the pale, doomed sots in fairytales?"

"No," Scarlet said resentfully. "I don't want that either. But I thought you said you were afraid."

"I am, but we must begin somewhere, yes?"

Scarlet fell silent, staring at him. The shirt lay forgotten in his lap and a slow, bright blush crept across his fair skin.

Liall wanted to smile but held it back, knowing it

would offend him. Poor Scarlet, he thought. You are no child, but sometimes I think you have no idea what effect you have on me, how one glance of you in your nightshirt, stretching and knuckling the sleep out of your eyes, can make me burn for you.

Liall often woke at night with the sharp scent of his own arousal in his nose and his member hard and moist on his belly, begging for notice. Attention he never gave it, for he was too aware of Scarlet being so near, sleeping next to him but inviolate as the moon through their mutual trust. He had a foolish fear that Scarlet would catch him pleasuring himself. It was a boy's fear, and silly. If Scarlet were any other man, he would not have hesitated to relieve himself whenever he needed to, albeit with a small amount of discretion, but this was Scarlet.

When Scarlet dressed, Liall would gaze hungrily for a flash of white limb being slid into the hateful clothing that hid it from him. He longed to claim that skin and cover it with kisses, to draw sighs of pleasure from Scarlet's lips and make him clutch at him and beg. Alas, still a dream. Aside from the brief embraces since they met up in Volkovoi, they had been as chaste as brothers with each other.

"What is the matter?" Liall pressed. "Do you not want to kiss me?"

"Yes," Scarlet answered at once.

"Then perhaps you no longer desire me?" he teased. "Have you changed your mind so quickly?"

Scarlet threw the shirt he was mending aside. "Don't be a want-wit!"

"Then perhaps you are ashamed of me. Too good to dirty yourself with a Kasiri."

Scarlet gaped at his unfairness. "Liall, I swear to you, that's not true at all."

Liall shrugged and left off watching Scarlet to give his

attention to the ceiling, watching the little flame on the smaller candle-lamp sway with the waves. After a few moments, Scarlet rose and came to sit beside him. Liall felt warm fingers threading with his and risked a look at Scarlet. A line of remorse was etched deep across Scarlet's forehead, and there was pain in his eyes

"Gods, look at you. I was only joking," Liall sighed. Scarlet was too young by far. He had known that from the moment they met. Scarlet had no experience in love or the complicated dance of power between couples, and Liall could have easily manipulated him. He might even gave done it, if not for his own guilt over the way they had met.

"I'm sorry," Scarlet said contritely. "I don't mean to make you feel..."

Liall sighed and put his fingers to Scarlet's lips. "Hush, the fault is mine." Yes, the fault is mine, he thought. It is a great responsibility for a man my age to take a lover so green and youthful, for I have the knowledge and skill to do you harm or manipulate you terribly, and I must never use it. I must protect you always. Yet... one kiss cannot hurt.

"No, it's not, I—"

Liall slipped his hand around the back of Scarlet's neck and pulled him closer. "I said," he repeated, his breath gusting over Scarlet's mouth. "Hush."

After the first heated touch of skin to skin, mouth to mouth, Scarlet exhaled in a shaking sigh and his tense body relaxed, sinking against Liall. Liall wound his arms around Scarlet and rolled on the bed until Scarlet was half under him. Liall's hand roamed over Scarlet's shoulders and stomach, snaking down to caress the warm line of his thigh.

"Liall," Scarlet whispered shakily, when he was allowed to breathe.

"Yes?" Liall murmured back, pressing Scarlet's body to him deliciously, loving the feel of him, the lean slenderness and wiry muscle contrasted by the incredible softness of his skin, the silk of his hair and the full, wet mouth. Scarlet was altogether intoxicating. Liall found himself rubbing against Scarlet's body like a cat, for that is what Scarlet reminded him of: a small, elegant cat with ready claws and sharp teeth. There was a fire building in Liall. It roared in his ears as he drowned his senses in the feel of Scarlet's mouth, the way his lips parted to allow Liall's tongue entrance, the way his legs opened sweetly to pillow Liall's hips.

Liall ground against him, pushing their bodies together, stoking the melting heat in his groin, clutching and thrusting, frantically close, so very close

"Liall!"

Liall jumped back like a shot, his heart thudding. "What?"

"Can't you hear me?"

"Hear what?" Liall wiped his mouth. He had been right on the verge, so close that the dull ache of unfulfilled passion scraped on his nerves like sand in an open wound. Scarlet's eyes were wide and his breathing ragged, and Liall recalled suddenly – and with some shame – that all was not as he had imagined in his ardor. Scarlet's legs hadn't opened to him: he had thrust them apart with his knee. Scarlet's mouth had yielded at last to his probing, but only after Liall nipped his lower lip and Scarlet yelped in surprise.

Liall looked away and recoiled to the edge of the bed, head down, breathing raggedly as he rebuilt his shattered composure. It was not easy. The same berserker rage that often took Rshani warriors into battle- madness made them intemperate lovers as well. Truly, he thought dizzily, there is a reason for our proper ways and fine speech: it hides the animal inside.

He reminded himself that Scarlet still had not realized how very unlike their races were, that the differences between Hilurin and Rshani ran deeper than skin and hair and the color of their eyes. They were a completely opposite species, at times as brutal and savage as Hilurin are aloof and cool, swift to temper and swifter to passion, and not all of it wholly controllable.

"Sorry, I'm sorry," Scarlet stammered. "I wanted you to, I just...I don't know what happened."

"I crave your pardon," Liall was able to say at last, though it stuck in his throat. His bed would remain empty for a while yet. Months, maybe. Oh, Scarlet was worth it, he knew. At that moment, however, his body knew no such thing.

Scarlet touched Liall's arm. "Liall—"

Liall jerked away. "Spare me your pity. I will not die if I do not have your touch."

"Are you all right?"

"It will pass."

"Are you sure, you look kind of—"

"Hell's teeth!" Liall stood up and whirled on him. "Either bed me or leave me alone, but cease your prattle! I cannot take any more of this!"

Scarlet's expression reflected shock and hurt, enough to make even a cruel man think twice, but Liall was beyond caring. He stormed to the door and flung it open. The icy blast that rushed in doused the candle and put a fresh damper on his lust, but not his temper.

"I need to walk before my head explodes!" he snarled. "Serves me right for taking up with a *boy!*"

Liall left, slamming the door behind him so loud that the timbers shook.

Scarlet sat rigidly as the cabin door had slammed, feeling very much as if Liall had struck him physically. Liall hinted at love, but would not say it. Liall asked for a kiss and then tried to take more than that, and when Scarlet refused, Liall dared to call him the child!

Slowly, Scarlet's hurt faded into anger. He began to suspect they each wanted very different things from each other: Liall seemed to want only pleasure, while Scarlet wanted much more than that. Still, he thought angrily, no matter how much I care for him, he has no right to push me into pleasing him, as if I were a whore.

Scarlet still harbored a horror of being viewed like the boys for sale in the souk: a pretty piece of meat, fit only for the bed or the block. When Liall refused to answer his questions, it only intensified his growing suspicion that Liall did not consider him a suitable mate.

A suitable bedmate, perhaps, he thought sourly. But still, have I been any more honest than he has? I've hinted and looked, but did I ever say I cared for him?

Cursing himself, Scarlet drew on his coat and gloves. Opening the abused door, he ducked out into the icy wind, shielding his eyes while trying to discern which way Liall went. Cold sleet drove out of a black sky, making his eyes water. He saw no sign of Liall near the inner railing, and the deck bucked worse than any Byzantur ferry ever had. He ventured out to the companionway, holding on to the wooden rails and shivering, and worked his way down the narrow walk. As he reached the end of it, he dimly recognized Liall standing braced by the bulward watching the sea churn, and Liall was not alone. The young mariner with the pale hair stood very close to

Liall. As Scarlet watched, the mariner took Liall's hand and bowed over it, pressing a kiss to Liall's skin.

The cold wind roared in Scarlet's ears and battered him. He had seen the mariner watching Liall with desire before.

As Scarlet stood, locked in hesitation of whether to stay or flee, he saw Liall's hand come up and briefly cup the young mariner's cheek. The mariner's eyes looked past Liall's shoulder and locked with Scarlet's momentarily, and the mariner smiled in gloating triumph.

Liall, seeing that his companion's gaze was elsewhere, turned and saw Scarlet watching them. Scarlet whirled around and quickly fought his way through the wind back to the cabin, his heart thudding.

Rutting bastard! Let him bed the stinking mariner if that's all he's after! He slammed the poor cabin door hard enough to rattle the frame and stood there shaking and breathing hard. Once inside, he felt trapped and angry.

The door opened and Liall was there. "Scarlet," he said, as he closed the door firmly behind him. "I do not know what you think, but—"

"It doesn't matter," he broke in, fighting to keep his voice steady. "Just don't say anything."

He turned his face to the wall for fear Liall could see how much he was affected, how much seeing Liall touch the mariner had wounded him. Whatever else, he did not want Liall to see him that way. Scarlet picked up his pack and sat with his back against the wall, pretending to mend a strong strap on the side that needed no mending, determined not to look at Liall.

After a long moment, Liall crossed the cabin toward him. Liall's fingers touched Scarlet's hair lightly. "Scarlet," he said, a note of chastisement in his voice. "I do not deny that Oleksei sought my company in his bed, but if you think I would cast you aside thus without even a word, you are mistaken."

Oleksei, Scarlet seethed. The name was alien and beautiful, nothing at all like his. He kept mute, afraid to say anything at all, for fear of shaming himself or making an already tangled matter worse. Liall sighed and muttered in Sinha, and then the bunk creaked as he lay down again.

Scarlet stayed awake for perhaps an hour after he heard Liall's breathing even out into the rhythm of sleep. Eventually, the rolling of the ship soothed his mind and he slept, waking only when a swell tossed the ship and he thumped his head hard against the cabin wall. He opened his eyes to darkness and tried to stand, finding he could not. The movement of the ship robbed him of any proper sense of direction. For a moment, he could not recall where he was, and then strong hands caught hold of him and an arm went around his waist, lifting him to his feet.

Still dazed and disoriented, he held on. The cabin was cold as death, and Scarlet realized he had let the fire burn out.

Liall's voice was close to his ear. "I have you," Liall rumbled, his voice as steady as the ship was not. "Are you all right?"

"Just bumped m'head," Scarlet said blearily. He blinked a few times in the utter blackness to clear his vision, and the corners of the cabin took shape in the form of blurred, silvery lines. He could see the bunk now, and the shape of Liall's body next to him.

"Do not move. I will find the lantern."

"I can see," Scarlet said.

"In this?" Liall's voice registered surprise. "How?"

Scarlet held on to Liall as another swell tipped the cabin alarmingly. Blind himself, Liall urged him over to the bunk. Scarlet lay down without protest, not even bothering to take off his boots, Liall settled into the bunk next to him and Scarlet huddled against the welcome warmth, wondering if Liall even felt the cold. He never seemed to, and certainly he never complained.

"Rough seas," Liall murmured. One strong arm curled around Scarlet's back, drawing him closer to Liall's chest.

Scarlet had a thought that Liall might be referring to more than the actual water. "Yes," he agreed quietly. He was glad Liall did not question him further about his sight. Most Hilurin have an innate ability to see well in dark, which accounts for much of their skill at navigating roads and rivers. It was just one more piece of evidence that pointed to how different he was from Liall, and how far apart their races were.

Liall placed his palm against Scarlet's face. "You're freezing," he commented, and tugged the heavy blanket up around them both.

"I fell asleep. The brazier burned out."

"We will light it again in the morning. This will do for now." He rubbed Scarlet's arms through the blankets.

Their hands brushed, and Scarlet felt Liall's fingers lacing with his. Liall's hands trembled a bit, and Scarlet realized suddenly that he was not the only one in this cabin who was worried and afraid. Liall carries his own set of fears, he thought, wondering. They may be different from mine, but not lesser.

He felt Liall press a quick, chaste kiss to his temple. "I am sorry for my behavior earlier. It will not happen again."

Scarlet wondered what he meant by that exactly. Wouldn't try to touch him again, or wouldn't get mad when he was refused?

"Go back to sleep," Liall whispered, lulling like the sea.

The next day was brief and bright, windy but without the fierce gales that had harried the ship northward for a solid week. Wind still caught in the huge white sails and filled them, driving the ship ever northwards, but the dim sun, a small, fuzzy ball of yellow light veiled in white mist, gave the illusion of warmth. With his red pedlar's coat buttoned tight, Scarlet found a spot on the deck to soak in it. Liall had told him they would soon be entering the Great North Sea, and once they were there, the sun would vanish entirely and shroud them in blue twilight that would not fade, but endure for months. Although Scarlet could not imagine a world without a sun, the ever-shortening days seemed to bear out the truth of Liall's words.

Liall was restless, working with the mariners when they would allow and helping with various chores. When he joined Scarlet on the deck at last, his mood was bored and out of sorts.

"Byzans are sun lizards," Liall said as he stood beside Scarlet. "Enjoy it while you can, for soon the sun will be a memory to us."

"If you say so," Scarlet muttered. "I still don't see how the world goes on without a sun. How do you know when to sleep?"

"You get used to it." Liall held out his hand. "Come, you need exercise. You learned knives from your travels in the caravan, you said? I saw some of that in the alley at Volkovoi, but you must show me what you can really do."

"The man who taught me was a not a master," Scarlet said as Liall grasped his hand and hauled him to his feet.

"Rannon was a good fighter, but I've never had any real training."

Liall nodded thoughtfully. "We will mend that lack in Rshan." He looked out over the sea. "Perhaps twenty days more and you will see the land of my birth. Rshan na Ostre, the Land of Night." He seemed depressed at the prospect.

Scarlet tugged his red woolen cap down around his ears as a gust of wind battered them. He was very aware of the mariners working nearby, many of whom had stopped to stare at him as he chatted with Liall.

Liall followed the direction of Scarlet's gaze and scowled at the staring crewmen. "There is a spot on the half deck that has been scraped clean of ice," he said. "We will practice there." He strode away, plainly expecting Scarlet to follow him at once.

Scarlet tagged after Liall uneasily, simply because there was nothing else to do and it seemed they would quarrel if he did not. An argument in front of the gawking crew did not appeal to him at the moment. Though Liall's high-handed attitude irritated him, he obeyed without complaint.

Liall borrowed four sparring long-knives – heavy but blunted – from Captain Qixa. The dour captain looked at Scarlet as if he doubted his ability to lift even one of the blades. Qixa exchanged several sentences with Liall in their incomprehensible language, ending with Qixa staring at Scarlet in surprise and disbelief.

Liall shot Scarlet a look. "He says you are too small, and I will cut you in half with this." Liall hefted the sparring knife and spun it a little in his hand. "I told him you saved my life in Volkovoi with a pair of Morturii knives."

"Does he believe you?"

Liall shrugged. "No."

They left the captain and moved to the half deck between the mast and the captain's cabin. The wind was still for the moment and a parade of clouds chased across the sky. Liall chose a spot and spun the blade in his hand again, testing their weight, before taking up a fighting stance. Scarlet stripped off his coat and laid it on the deck.

Liall began first, lunging in with his right to distract while holding the left blade in reserve, ready to slip past Scarlet's knives. Scarlet guarded warily, turning to protect his vulnerable left side. After a rough beginning, Rannon's fighting lessons came back to Scarlet, and he returned each of Liall's moves with fluid counterstrikes.

"You have talent!" Liall called out. He seemed pleased and was not at all winded.

"Not so poor as you expected?"

Liall attacked with his left knife, not as swift as Scarlet knew he could, and Scarlet battered him back. He liked watching Liall, who moved with startling grace for such a large man, and who was careful to test him without endangering either of them. Scarlet danced away from the edge of Liall's knife and they traded blows, circling each other, for several minutes.

At last, Liall called a halt, raising his hand. "Are you tired?"

Scarlet shook his head impatiently and feinted with his right-hand blade, causing Liall's mouth to twitch into a grim smile. They began again, swifter this time, Liall less worried about Scarlet's skill and more eager to push him to his limits, testing him. They sparred for more than an hour, until the breath heaved in Scarlet's lungs and the muscles of his right arm began to tremble.

He knew it was unwise to keep going, but he was unwilling to say he'd had enough. When a counterstrike came dangerously close to Scarlet's throat, he thought

Liall would stop immediately, but Liall was lost in the pleasure of movement and did not see Scarlet's weariness. Liall pressed forward as Scarlet dropped his guard.

The sun was setting, and the reddish haze was reflected off the edge of Liall's knife into Scarlet's eyes. For one instant, the sight threw Scarlet back to a time before Lysia was burned, when a bandit Kasiri had held him pinned and helpless in the snow with the point of a dagger at his throat: a dagger that caught the red light and flashed it into his eyes.

Liall froze. "Scarlet?"

Scarlet blinked to clear his vision of phantoms. "I'm sorry, my arm—"

Liall's face changed. "You are tired. I did not see it." He took a step forward and bent to pick up the fallen knife as Scarlet got to his feet.

Scarlet flinched and backed up too quickly. His boot heel caught a ridge in the deck and he tripped, his rump hit the deck, and the knife fell from his right hand and landed with a muted clang.

Once on his feet, Scarlet looked away from Liall in embarrassment, ashamed of his weakness. Liall's brief good mood had evaporated.

"I frightened you," Liall said.

Scarlet nodded. He felt like he should apologize, but knew it would be unwelcome. He could only gaze at Liall's hard, set face in distress.

"Do not... what is it you say? Don't vex yourself," Liall said. "It happens to the best of soldiers. You were only remembering. It is nothing."

Scarlet realized Liall believed he was flashing back to the pirate battle. "I'm sorry."

"For what? You have done nothing. Shall we return these blades to the captain? The sun will be down soon, and all our warmth gone if we stand here."

Scarlet gathered up his coat and handed his blunted knives to Liall. "Will I improve, you think?"

"You will," Liall said with certainty.

"Can we spar again sometime?"

"I think not," Liall answered curtly, avoiding his eyes.

"Why?"

"Stop chattering," Liall ordered. "Come."

Liall lead them back to the captain's cabin in silence, and Scarlet snuck a look at the hard lines of Liall's profile. I've offended him somehow, he thought, but he could not recall a single thing he had done.

Qixa was not in his cabin. Liall pointed to the aft. "You will return to the cabin. I need to speak with Qixa on another matter."

Scarlet nodded. "All right."

"And do not speak to the crew," Liall warned.

"Wasn't planning on it," Scarlet said sourly before turning away, and he had the brief satisfaction of seeing Liall's composure crack a little before turning away.

5.

Malice

Liall negotiated his way up the slippery wooden steps to the quarterdeck where Qixa was stationed. The captain was grimly staring at the gray horizon as if he could intimidate it, a brass spyglass clenched in his beefy hands.

Liall's thoughts were as shaky as his feet were steady. Scarlet had tired easily, but he fought well and his mind had been on target, watching Liall's body and anticipating each move and turn. For Liall's part, the match had been vastly different. He sparred with Scarlet out of habit, his limbs moving almost automatically. Other thoughts occupied the dark spaces in his brain, the corners he seldom touched, and they all whispered to him of the same fear, the same prayer: *Do not let me love this boy.*

The argument had been ridiculous. It was the sort of thing one might read in love stories, wherein two tortured lovers clawed and tore at each other's addled sensibilities on their fumbling parade toward the mating-bed.

I am, Liall supposed, the bridegroom in all this, though I feel more like the fool. What will they make of such an innocent in Rshan? I have told him that the mariners are dangerous, but I have said nothing of what we will face once we make landfall. Is that wisdom on my part, or merely cowardice?

Then Scarlet had tripped and fallen backwards and the point of Liall's blade had been suddenly close to Scarlet's throat, and for one instant, madness ruled Liall's soul. He thought it would be wise to kill the Hilurin now, before they came to Rshan, and before any more damage could be done to either of them.

They will tear him apart, Liall had thought in a kind of near-panic as Scarlet looked up at him from the deck. And through him, you. Save yourself. Save him.

Liall's focus had narrowed down to the sight of his hand clenched around the hilt of the sparring blade. Move, hand, he commanded it. It would not, and he comprehended with dull resignation that it was already far too late.

He had dropped his stance, helped Scarlet to stand and apologized to him, and then sent him off to the cabin with a muttered excuse about finding Qixa.

As Liall approached, Qixa fitted a long spyglass to his eye and stared south, his lips peeled back from his teeth as if snarling at the waves.

"Something amiss?"

Qixa lowered the glass and handed it to Liall. "See for yourself."

Liall gazed through the lens for several moments. There was little to see. A misty fog hovered over the wave caps and limited their visibility to about three hundred feet. It had been the same yesterday. "Nothing," Liall said, offering the instrument back. He watched Qixa wrap his hands around the smooth brass barrel of the spyglass. "Your nose tells you otherwise?"

Qixa nodded shortly. "Aye."

Qixa said nothing more, and Liall knew without needing to be told that Qixa had offered a mariner's instinct: there was danger ahead that Qixa could not see, but only sensed. Liall had been warned.

He bowed respectfully to Qixa, equal to equal, and left the quarterdeck, the sparring blades still in his hands.

He had forgotten about returning them.

Once Liall was out of sight, Scarlet slowed and moved more carefully across the deck, which was still patchy with ice. He crossed a short expanse with delicate steps, mindful of losing his balance, then continued with more confidence. The main deck had gathered more ice while he was away, and just before he reached the cabin, he slipped and his back hit the deck, hard. All the breath was driven out of his lungs, and he barely felt the wind tear his coat from his fingers. The coat rose up briefly and twisted before his eyes like a red bird before fluttering away toward the bow. Above him, the gray sky whirled like a pinwheel and a few brilliant spots of light danced before his eyes. I will not pass out, he told himself sternly, and forced his lungs to work, to inhale.

He heard a man's laughter nearby, but could not summon the dignity to care. Resigned to being mocked, Scarlet rolled over and tried to clamber upright, his boots sliding on ice. Suddenly, two big hands pulled him to his feet and drove his arms against his middle.

Scarlet craned his neck to see who held him and glimpsed that it was Oleksei, who had often cast lustful glances at Liall.

It surprised him very much that this one should help him, but only for a moment, until Oleksei clamped a hand over his mouth and another arm over his chest. Even then, Scarlet did not begin to truly fight until Oleksei began to haul him away from the cabin. It was shock that held him back, and then fear slipped into his veins and gave him strength. Later, he would pride himself that he blackened both the mariner's eyes by slamming his head back hard enough to feel the man's nose crunch against the back of his skull.

Oleksei's fist hit him on the back of his neck and Scarlet went down, the world graying out around him. Dimly, he watched as Oleksei kicked open a nearby lower hatchway, then everything was spinning air and darkness as he was hauled over and dropped into the hold. He landed hard and only managed to scramble to his knees before his arms were seized. Someone grabbed him again from behind, clamped a hard, filthy hand over his mouth and bent him face first over one of the wide barrels that the mariners used to carry fresh water in.

Though biting is not honorable, Scarlet turned his head and bit hard into the thumb pressed against his mouth. Warm blood broke over his teeth and flowed over his tongue, and the mariner roared and jerked his hand away. A hammer-like blow to the back of his head made his ears ring and his vision turn dark and smoky, and he slumped over the barrel in a daze.

Too stunned to shout for help or even to move, he moaned as blows rained down on his back and shoulders, and it began to dawn on him that this was more than simple lust. This was spite.

Fear roused him enough to stir, for he sensed murder in the air, and then there were two bodies holding him while someone's hands fought to tear his breeches down. Panic gave him a last burst of strength and he broke free once and kicked backward, hearing a man grunt in pain. A hand pressed down on the back of Scarlet's neck, fingers hard as stone, and ground his face against the rough, splintered wood. Heavy boots kicked at his calves, pushing his legs wider apart, and a mariner's hands – probably Oleksei's – worked the laces of his breeches loose, jerking and tearing. Cold air rushed over his bare skin, and there was a rough whisper in his ear, the silken brush of long golden strands against his cheek.

"Lenilyn whore," Oleksei hissed. His fingers pressed between the cheeks of Scarlet's rump, probing crudely.

Pinned down, Scarlet whimpered and considered begging, as he had once considered begging Cadan for his life. Then, as now, he knew that it would be useless.

Then Oleksei's weight was suddenly lifted off him. There was a loud crash and a rising chorus of shouts. Scarlet did not hesitate, but tore his wrists out of the mariner's grasp and fell to the floor on the other side of the barrel.

Liall stood under the hatchway, the dying sunlight turning his white hair to red gold. He held the sparring blade and he was raging at mariners in his native tongue. The point of his blade, sharp enough to puncture though all the edges were blunted, was pressed to Oleksei's throat.

Scarlet groped to his feet, shaking and holding his breeches up with one hand. Liall's pale blue eyes snapped to him. "Move."

Scarlet braced himself against the crate and limped over to stand behind Liall.

Liall's voice was cold with rage. "What say you, Scarlet? Does he die?"

"No," he croaked, and licked his lips. He tasted blood and touched his lower lip to find it swollen and split.

Another figure dropped into the hold. Scarlet tensed when he saw it was the quartermaster, but the man took up stance beside Liall, holding a short dueling knife out toward the mariners. The quartermaster regarded his men with displeasure and barked orders in Sinha.

Liall glanced at Scarlet briefly. "No?"

"No," he repeated, conscious of the quartermaster's eyes on him. "I'm alive. I don't want any more deaths on my conscience."

That got him a curious look from the quartermaster, and Scarlet realized that the man did indeed speak Bizye.

"I think it a mistake," Liall said, his eyes on Oleksei, "to let this man live. If he crosses me again, I will surely kill him." He looked at the quartermaster. "You will deal with this," he commanded.

The quartermaster nodded shortly and beckoned to Scarlet to follow him. When Scarlet did not move, Liall grabbed his arm and pulled him aside to let another mariner jump down into the hold. Liall handed the second mariner his blade and knelt to give Scarlet a lift up.

"I can do it myself—" Scarlet began.

"You cannot," Liall snapped. "Do as I say."

He put his boot in Liall's hand and Liall boosted him high enough to grip the edge of the hatch. To his surprise, Qixa himself was there. The captain reached down to haul him up to the deck.

Scarlet peered down into the hatch, waiting for Liall to follow, but Qixa shook his head.

"He will come soon," the captain said gruffly in passable Bizye, taking Scarlet's arm.

"My thanks," Scarlet said, trying to step back from him. Qixa's iron grip held him fast. "I can walk on my own." He felt warmth sliding down his neck and realized his face was bleeding heavily.

Qixa eyed him for a moment before letting go, but walked behind him until they reached the cabin. The wind had turned bitterly cold and the red light of the sunset seemed to mock Scarlet's every halting step. He wanted to rage at someone or something, to lash out and strike, but there was no target for his fury. The only person Scarlet wanted to attack was Oleksei, and he was no match for the mariner. That had already been proven.

Qixa opened the cabin door for him, and Scarlet

slipped inside. He closed it in Qixa's face and leaned his back against it for a moment, then limped over to huddle on the bed. Tremors wracked his body and he was aware of the steady drip of blood onto the floor. He was still shaking when Liall arrived with a basin of water and a clean cloth, his mouth drawn down into a hard sketch of anger. A bared, razor-sharp long-knife was in his other hand.

Liall put the basin on the floor and sat down next to him very carefully. He had to clear his throat before speaking. "How badly are you hurt?"

"Not very." Scarlet's hands were still clutching his middle, holding together the closure of his breeches.

Liall made to put his hand there. "Let me—"

"No!" Scarlet jerked away from him. "They did not."

"No?" Liall sagged in relief. "I thought…if I had been only a little later."

"They did not," Scarlet repeated. "It didn't happen. It's over, just like…"

Liall put his arm around him with great care. "Just like?"

"Cadan," he said simply.

Liall's head bowed. He closed his eyes tightly and uttered a curse. "I am overjoyed that you killed him. I hope it was painful and very slow."

"I remembered your dagger in my boot when they were holding me down," Scarlet went on, still stunned, his words slow and halting. "The others… I think it frightened them, all the blood. They were not expecting that any of them would die that day, and so I escaped that time, too."

Liall made a noise of disgust.

Scarlet despaired suddenly as all the terror and pain seemed to catch up with him at once. "Is the whole world like this, Liall?" he asked plaintively. A drop of blood splashed on the back of his hand. He wiped his face and then stared at the swath of bright red painted across his skin. The splintered wood of the water barrel had caught and cleanly torn the skin over his right cheekbone, leaving him with a long wound just under his eye.

Liall reached for the basin and knelt on the floor in front of Scarlet. He carefully cleaned the cut with a wet cloth while on his knees before the pedlar. It was deep.

"Oleksei has scarred you," he said lowly. "I will cut off his hands for it."

There were hard lines of fury around Liall's mouth.

Scarlet shook his head. "No."

"No? Why should I spare that pig?"

"Because," Scarlet said tiredly "it's not justice to demand death for insult, a pair of hands for a cut on my pretty face. That's revenge."

"Do you not deserve revenge?"

Scarlet hesitated. "Maybe. But I don't want it. Not that way."

Liall gritted his teeth. "But why?"

"Deva wouldn't approve. And besides, it's not honorable. I shouldn't send another man to do what I can't do myself."

"I do not share your sense of honor. You know this."

"That's why you were so mad at me that last day, when you cut the dress off me."

Liall froze at the mention of that dawn in the Kasiri camp when he and Scarlet had come to blows.

It was the culmination of a struggle that began between them when Liall had demanded a kiss in payment for the toll and Scarlet had refused. After several other tricks had failed, Scarlet had dressed in his mother's clothes and tried to sneak by the Wolf. Liall had not been fooled, and had laughingly cut the costume from the pedlar's body, scalding Scarlet's pride and leading him to call Liall a rapist and a probable murderer. Liall had reacted so badly that Scarlet had feared he would die.

"I was no better, I admit it. I frightened you and tried to break your pride," Liall said, his mouth twisting as if he would spit. His hands were gentle as a woman's, "It was not the battle you were remembering on the deck today. It was me."

"Liall—"

"No, I know. I was cruel to you when we first met. I was," Liall took a deep, controlled breath. "No more talk. We must see to your injuries."

Scarlet's teeth were chattering. "How did you find me?"

"I found your coat on the deck," Liall explained. "You would never have just left it there. Not you. You're too neat and you hate the cold too much. I knew you had to be in trouble." He clucked his tongue in distress and dropped the bloodied cloth into the basin. "There's so much blood on your clothes. Let me clean you up and get you warm, *t'aishka*."

Scarlet did not have the strength to argue. T'aishka. The word sounded exotic, but pleasing. He tried to pronounce it and failed, and saw the flicker in Liall's eyes at his rude attempt at the word. "What does that word mean?"

Liall did not smile, but his gaze was strange and powerful. "I will tell you some day when... when you are as certain as I am. I am certain now, and that is enough for me to say it."

Crouching, Liall rinsed the cloth in the bloody basin and carefully began to wash the rest of Scarlet's face, his expression stony. Scarlet noticed Liall's hands had a noticeable tremor.

"I'm not hurt bad," Scarlet said, touched.

"I know, but I am angry. You must allow me that. You were angry in Volkovoi, no?"

He had been, and had wanted to kill the bravo on the edge of his blade. Liall nodded and he cleaned more of Scarlet's face and throat, then helped him out of the shirt and fetched a clean blanket from the cedar chest.

Liall then made him raise his arms and take several deep breaths. "No pain when you breathe inward? Good. You chest is only bruised, then," he pronounced. "They look nearly as bad, I do assure you. Oleksei will lose his thumb, most likely: it is bitten almost clean through. You did very well, Scarlet."

"Oleksei," Scarlet said, shivering as he wrapped up in the blanket. "I wish I didn't know his name. That makes it worse, somehow. It's hard to hate a nameless thing."

Liall gave him a strange look, and something passed between them. He nodded a little, his eyes shadowed. "Yes, Oleksei, curse him. But I never desired him. I swear that to you." He began to clean a small cut on Scarlet's wrist. "When cornered, you are as fierce as a snow bear. They expected you to submit tamely."

"Their mistake."

Liall's fingers cleaned the cut delicately. "I could have warned them, stubborn lad," he said, striving for a teasing note. It fell flat.

Scarlet had stopped shivering when a knock sounded at the hatch. Liall jumped up, reaching for his knives. The door opened at Liall's call, revealing the quartermaster and another mariner who carried a covered tray. The quartermaster bowed slightly and spoke to Liall in his own language, then switched to Bizye, looking at Scarlet.

"The captain recommends that you eat something hot, ser, and has sent both a salve for the bruises and some herbs to help you sleep, if there is... pain."

Liall watched him from beneath lowered brows.

"There will be no pain of that kind," he growled. "And well it is so, or there would be three dead men tonight."

The quartermaster bowed again and spoke respectfully. Liall snapped something back and the two mariners withdrew. Liall bolted the door when they had gone.

"What was that about?"

"Idiots," he said, and sat down on the bunk beside Scarlet. "You must eat all of this soup. You look better now that your illness has passed, but you need to put a bit of fat on that frame or you will freeze in Rshan, the land that does not exist." He winked.

The soup was good and the che was bland but hot. Scarlet suspected that Liall put some of the herbs in after all, because he was sleepy after, but comfortably so.

"Will you let me have a look at you?" Liall asked with worry. "There might be further injuries under your clothes, where I could not see. Or I could send for the curae again," he offered.

Scarlet made a sound of distaste. "Gods, no. Not him." He hesitated, and then began to toe off his boots and remove his breeches, blushing with embarrassment. "I fell on the ice, before...just before. And then he threw me into the hold. I don't know what I landed on."

Liall's face was troubled as he politely looked away. Scarlet finished undressing and pulled the blanket around him before Liall motioned for Scarlet to lie down on his stomach.

Liall's touch was gentle as he rubbed the salve into a blue bruise high on Scarlet's shoulder. Scarlet was tense for several minutes, and then, as his heart slowed and the after-effects of panic set in, his muscles relaxed and he nearly dozed.

He stirred when he felt hands at his waist and started awake, heart pounding, but Liall whispered reassurance into his ear.

"I was only seeing if your legs were cut," Liall murmured. "I would leave it, but I fear infection on this ship."

Scarlet nodded wearily. "No, that's wise, I suppose. The hold was filthy."

Liall's expression was grave. "Please excuse me."

Scarlet sighed and closed his eyes, resting his torn cheek against the cover. It continued to ooze blood steadily. "I'm getting the sheets bloody."

"Let it bleed," Liall advised. "Perhaps it will help it to heal faster if the blood washes the poison away."

His face hurt more than any of the rest of his injuries, for the moment. Scarlet heard Liall hiss as the blanket was moved aside. He raised his head, craning to see. "Bad?" he asked.

"They were excessive," Liall said through his teeth. "If they did not intend to kill you, you could not prove it from this."

Scarlet decided not to look after all. The salve set warmth glowing on the bruised spots on his lower back, easing them, and he was surprised at how many spots there were as Liall carefully applied it. Later, he would find a blackened bruise the size of his fist on his calf, where Oleksei had kicked him.

"They are fortunate indeed that you were more calm than me," Liall said, his voice low and frightening.

"I didn't feel very calm at the time," he mumbled sleepily.

Liall tugged the blankets loosely around Scarlet. "They are fortunate," he said stonily. "They laid hands on someone I... care about, intending to harm."

Liall's words were like balm to Scarlet, far soothing than the medicine. *He cares about me.* His head was buzzing with all the thoughts that were packed into it, like bees in a jar.

Liall smeared the salve liberally on a clean piece of linen and had Scarlet press it to his torn face. "Try to sleep with it there," he advised as he set the salve aside, rinsed his hands in the water left in the basin and kicked off his boots. He took a blanket and made a rough bed on the floor next to the bunk, his knives within easy reach. "Sleep, t'aishka. Nothing will disturb you further tonight. I swear it."

Days passed, and as Liall's initial fear that Scarlet's wounds would become infected faded, Liall seemed consumed with his commitment to punish Oleksei and the mariner's conspirators. The quartermaster took a vote among the crew, and it was agreed the ones who attacked Scarlet should be whipped. Scarlet gathered there was some dissent over that, but it was mostly from Liall, who wanted the men branded as well, and also a few of the more vocal mariners who disagreed with the sentence and wanted a much lighter punishment. There was a day when Liall's mood was like a black sky and even to speak to him was risking a cloudburst. Scarlet found out later that it was because Oleksei and his men claimed that Scarlet had promised to whore for them. Oleksei asserted that Scarlet had taken their silver but refused them when the time came, so he and his men had only tried to take what they were due. The lie proved to be short-lived, for Liall offered trial by combat to determine the truth, and two of the men recanted. Scarlet supposed they came to their senses and reasoned a whipping was better than death.

Liall would have had Scarlet go up on deck to watch the whipping, but he refused. The atya shook his head at the strangeness of Byzans and went out to watch alone as the mariners were flogged. Scarlet could hear the whip strokes and the outcry anyway, so staying in the cabin did not shield him entirely from what was done. Liall came back pleased and did not understand why the punishment of his would-be rapists had affected Scarlet so.

"If they had succeeded in their crime," Liall informed coldly "I would have had them castrated. It is well for them that we are at sea, and they are needed to complete our journey."

"You don't understand," Scarlet said in shame. "You and the crew decided their punishment. That's justice, and I agree. But Deva forbids revenge, and I wouldn't be able to watch Oleksei being whipped without feeling happy about it."

Liall sighed. "I do not comprehend the difference. You have a right to want to see him punished."

"Yes," Scarlet agreed. "And no." He waved his hand and turned away. "I said you wouldn't understand."

Scarlet was wary of leaving the cabin after the whipping, fearing that the crew would want vengeance for their fellows, but Liall was always with him, and oddly, he was treated with more respect. Not surprisingly, one of the three who were flogged was the fellow who had put the coin down Scarlet's shirt.

When Scarlet pointed that out, Liall went stony-faced and quiet and vanished for an hour. When he returned, he looked grimly satisfied and would answer no questions. Liall also treated him with more respect and not so much like an unruly child, perhaps because he saw how much the mariners were already bruised and marked before they were flogged. When he mentioned this, Liall seemed upset.

"Those are not my reasons," Liall said.

"What, then?"

They were on the deck in the icy wind, the faint sun a pinpoint of brightness in the dawn mist. Liall took his hand and touched the healing cut under Scarlet's right eye. "Because I finally realized that fighting against what is happening between us is futile, t'aishka. What should be, shall be. It was decided long ago, and there is nothing that either of us can do."

Scarlet was curious, but when pressed, Liall would speak no more.

Three days later, in a wet, driving wind that Liall called 'brisk' but which stole Scarlet's breath away, Qixa ordered the men to gather fish that would sustain them until the end of their voyage.

"Further north the fish dwell deeper. Harder to catch," Liall explained, almost shouting over the wind. "We must take them now."

"How far away are we?" Scarlet asked, teeth chattering. The wind contained little needles of sleet and ice, and the sea boiled with foam . A gust nearly blew him off his feet and he clung to the ropes. Liall steadied him.

"Less than ten days, as Qixa reckons it, but it is the most dangerous leg of our journey, and many things can happen on those waters. We could easily be delayed or locked in ice. It is best to stop one day and get the fish while we can than to push on and take our chances with starvation."

While Liall and Scarlet stood on the heaving quarterdeck and watched, the mariners dumped long, tarred ropes into the icy waters, laying them out behind them in a swath leagues long. After an hour or so, the captain ordered the anchor dropped and they began to haul the ropes up over the rail, and Scarlet saw that the ropes were baited at intervals with chunks of fish and palm-sized hooks. They brought up ten hooks in a row with nothing, and then, on the eleventh, a fish as large as a dog with fins like scalloped sails tumbled over the rail in a flash of slippery silver.

They took two more before Liall's restlessness won out and he took the short steps to the main deck as the crew was hauling their fourth beast in. It had fearsome black eyes, fins as long as a man's arm, and shining, iridescent skin like an opal catfish. Scarlet had never seen the like and could not name the thing, but Liall laughed as he helped gaff the thing's mouth and called over his shoulder to Scarlet.

"It is called a wave-rider!" Liall shouted over the sound of the sea. The fish twisted nearly in half and turned its massive head toward Liall, and Scarlet gasped and started forward, but Liall only laughed. "No fear, it has no teeth!"

Perhaps not, but it could still dump Liall overboard! But Liall was sure-footed as a goat on the icy deck and Scarlet began to feel idle and useless to be standing there easy while they worked. He knew if he went down that Liall would be angry and order him away, so he stood with his hands folded on the rail and watched. It turned out to be pleasant watching: Liall's muscles strained under his woolen shirt as his body moved effortlessly into the rhythm of labor. He glanced up at Scarlet once, and his teeth flashed in his dark, handsome face when he grinned widely and waved.

So caught up was Scarlet in the scene below that he did not hear footsteps approaching from the wheel. By the time he had turned, Oleksei was standing next to him. Scarlet's heart froze over for a moment and he looked down quickly to see if Oleksei held a knife, but no, they were empty. Oleksei stared at him with hate, and Scarlet remembered where he was. Oleksei didn't have him in a stinking hold with a gang of mariners to hold him down, and there was a pair of Morturii knives hanging from his belt. The beating of his heart slowed and he met Oleksei's gaze without fear.

"Get away from me, you pig."

Oleksei held up his mangled thumb – the one Scarlet had bitten – and turned it into an obscene gesture. Scarlet looked aside and tried to step around Oleksei, but the mariner blocked him again.

"Lenilyn slut," Oleksei's voice was filled with loathing. "You may have your master fooled, but I know what you are. How much did you sell yourself for in Volkovoi?"

Scarlet would not answer the accusations of a rapist.

"So you do speak my language."

Oleksei spat. "The tongue of outlander filth. How he bears to speak it, I do not know."

Scarlet's lip curled, and he felt in himself a rising sense of power. Oleksei's hate had a basis deeper than simply loathing Scarlet's race, and realizing it somehow made Oleksei smaller in his eyes. "You want him," Scarlet said, lingering on the feeling of power. "You want him for yourself, but he doesn't know you're alive. It's me he wants, not you. That's why you hate me."

Oleksei skated his hand over empty air, as if thrusting away the idea. "You cloud his eyes with tribal magic," he accused. "As your kind has done to us before."

Scarlet laughed shortly, but a sliver of icy fear wormed into his heart. So far, no one, not even Liall, knew about his Gift, and he wanted to keep it that way. He gazed at Oleksei, wondering if he had guessed it or seen something during the pirate battle, but no, the man was fishing in the dark, using any bigotry or excuse to explain

Liall's incomprehensible attraction to a filthy lenilyn. It was corroded desire and bitterness behind Oleksei's accusation, not knowledge. Suddenly, the mariner was pathetic to him, and he felt a rush of satisfaction in being able to stare Oleksei down and know that there was absolutely nothing Oleksei could do to change how Liall felt about Scarlet. Oh, there was a knack to this tangle of desire. Instead of groping blindly in the dark, he was finally beginning to find his way.

"Take your bitterness and go, Oleksei. Choke on it."

Oleksei grinned unpleasantly. "He told you my name."

"Only so he could curse it."

Oleksei's smile died as his face twisted with hate. He made a grab for Scarlet's arm and missed when Scarlet stepped back quickly.

"You are safe on this voyage, tribal whore," Oleksei snarled. "But one day he will cast you off. You will be exiled back to the Brown Lands, and you will have to cross this sea to get there. I will be waiting for you."

What Scarlet might have answered was lost, for Liall was suddenly there, shoving Oleksei away from him so hard that the mariner fell and toppled to the deck. As large as Oleksei was, Liall was older and stronger and – Scarlet knew – a better fighter.

"Va!" Liall raged further in Sinha and spat, towering over Oleksei. Liall watched Oleksei climb to his feet before turning to Scarlet. His voice was much quieter. "Did he threaten you? What did he say?"

"Nothing that matters." Oleksei's insults were bad enough the first time, and Scarlet did not want them repeated. Scarlet took Liall's arm and leaned against him a little. The knowledge that his actions would gall Oleksei made him shameless, and he brushed his uninjured cheek against Liall's sleeve. "It's getting late, are you ready to go to bed yet?"

Liall stared at him for only a second longer than normal. "Certainly," he murmured, and with a last glare at Oleksei, he led Scarlet away.

Scarlet could feel Oleksei's eyes on his back for a long time. When they arrived at the cabin, he began to regret his brazenness. Perhaps Liall had taken him at his word and would expect... what? Funny, he thought. A month ago I would have done anything to get Liall to touch me, now... I don't know what to do.

Liall smiled dryly. "I know very well who your words were for. I expect nothing."

"I didn't mean to tease..." Scarlet began.

"Yes, you did," Liall said, dropping his coat off his shoulders. He pulled his shirt over his head and tossed it to the chair, reaching for his belt buckle. "But I do not mind a *little* teasing."

As Scarlet watched Liall undress, he realized that perhaps Liall was the one teasing. Liall kicked his boots off and pushed his breeches off his legs, and there he stood, a tall statue of amber skin and carved muscle. His chest was broad and hairless, his waist flat and ribbed with hard planes of muscle, and lower...

Scarlet could feel his face burning and he looked away quickly when he discovered that Liall was pale-haired all over. Deva, he was well-made! Beautiful, if such can be said of men. Seeing Liall, he realized it could.

"You do not enjoy looking at me?" Liall asked softly. He made no move to cover his body or get into bed, but rested one hand on his hip languidly. "Am I pleasurable to look on?"

"Yes," Scarlet admitted lowly. The scent of salt was heavy and his breath misted in front of his face as he exhaled shakily. The cabin was freezing, but Liall was born for this weather and seemed not to feel the cold.

"Very pleasurable."

"Then why look away?"

Scarlet took an unsteady breath. "Because you will laugh at me."

"Why?" Liall pressed, direct but simple.

"Because I don't know what to do," Scarlet blurted, his eyes nailed to the floor. Oh, Deva, he's going to think me a moron...

He heard Liall approach and felt warm hands on his shoulders.

"And why should you know?" Liall's voice was low and charged. "You think I would despise you for innocence? Scarlet, look at me."

Scarlet would not raise his head, not until Liall fitted a hand under his chin and urged him.

"Scarlet," Liall's voice caressed him like the warm fingers on his cheek. "You have no lack to be ashamed of."

Scarlet wished he could believe this, but too much had been drummed into his head. "I feel just like what Kio called me: a stuffy old Hilurin."

"Kio does not know you like I do." Liall pushed Scarlet's black hair – which was growing long – off his forehead.

"There is nothing in the least stuffy about you."

Scarlet looked away again, extremely uncomfortable. Liall sighed before releasing him. After a moment, Liall turned and folded his long frame into the bed. "What did Oleksei really say to you?"

"I can handle Oleksei," Scarlet answered boldly.

"No doubt." Liall pulled the covers up to his neck and rolled over, letting the matter drop.

A wave boomed against the hull and Scarlet sighed, his breath steaming in the cold air as he began to undress. When he climbed in beside Liall, the man pretended to be asleep. Scarlet wondered if it was kindness.

6.

T'aishka

"Liall, did I hear you say this was good for us?"

"Quite good. First rule of travel: make friends with your new climate."

"I don't think it wants to be f-friends," Scarlet stuttered, his teeth chattering.

They were getting very close to Rshan. The Ostre Sul had passed through the Circle – the invisible line drawn on maps that terminated the normal spans of day and night – twelve days ago. The farther north they drew, the less light they saw, and all was shrouded in a gray nothingness in which there was no sun and no stars. There was nothing to steer by this far into the cold seas, no landmark or constellation in the bland sky, only the compass needle by the helm that arrowed the ship dead north for weeks. Liall watched Scarlet observe this change in the sky and saw how it frightened him, but when the pedlar began speaking of disasters and portents, Liall demonstrated the celestial mechanics of the event with a lighted candle and a ball of wax, showing Scarlet how the light could only shine on certain parts of the ball during the year. After that, Scarlet relaxed and ceased viewing the sky with trepidation, though he did wonder often and aloud how they managed to keep their feet on the ground if the world was spinning as Liall claimed. He also wanted to know what the stars were, and if they had worlds that circled their warming light as Nemerl did, and what manner of people lived here, but to these, Liall had no answers.

It was freezing on deck, the air biting as fangs, and Scarlet shivered even under the heavy coat he was bundled into. His hands were gloved with thick, fur-lined leather and his arms were wrapped around his body, and still his slight frame rattled with shivers. Each new gale stole his breath away and clawed tears from his eyes. Scarlet bore it all without complaint, grinning at Liall over the high neckline as he blew his warm breath down into the coat's shell, conserving as much heat as possible.

"I am not trying to be cruel," Liall said over the sound of the wind. "I am exposing your blood to the temperature. It is far colder than this in Rshan during the winter months, and I do not know how long we will be there. The same is done with children."

"I'm not your child," Scarlet said immediately, with faint annoyance.

But Liall was afraid. Scarlet was already dangerously weakened by the voyage and his earlier sickness, not to mention the beating he had taken. Liall feared that if some measure was not taken to strengthen Scarlet, he would fall prey to the first illness that came along.

An extended gust blew over them, pushing chunks of slushy ice against the hull, and Scarlet began to shiver uncontrollably. Liall reached inside his coat and produced a silver flask that he had kept warm near his skin. Tipping off the cap, he took a swallow before handing it to Scarlet. Scarlet stared at it and seemed about to refuse, but Liall pushed it into his hands with a stern look.

Scarlet sighed and lifted the flask from Liall's fingers. He took one small sip and tried to give it back, his eyes widening at sharp burn of strong liquor, but Liall nudged his hand.

"Again. For true this time, you drink like a little girl."

Liall knew that would goad his pride, and true to form,

Scarlet tipped the flask up and took a mouthful too large even for a Northman.

Scarlet's eyes went very wide as he forcibly swallowed it down and then gasped for air. He swore in Falx and shook his head like his brains had been rattled.

Liall knew Scarlet's tongue must feel like cinders. That was the beauty of Rshan liquors: they were all made from the strongest spices or herbs and were very potent. Liall patted Scarlet's back helpfully as the young man gasped for breath, trying not to feel too sorry for him.

When Scarlet could breathe, he thrust the flask back at Liall. "There, happy now? Did I pass your damn test?"

Liall laughed and shook his head. "One more." Scarlet looked doubtful and angry at the same time. "It will warm you," he promised.

"Oh, warm," Scarlet answered glibly. "I remember being warm."

"And I remember you used to smile," Liall teased, pressing him to take one more drink.

In a few days they would arrive in Rshan. So far, the voyage had been one protracted song of disaster, danger, petty arguments and boredom. In the time since Oleksei and his fellows had attacked Scarlet, the pedlar had grown distant. When he slept beside Liall in the bunk, he was as close to the bulkhead as he could get without being on the other side, his back turned. Although the crew had begun to treat Scarlet with some respect since the pirate attack, his smiles had become rarer than the sun and he no longer laughed or joked with Liall at all.

Scarlet took another drink, a judiciously smaller one this time, turning the sharp taste over in his mouth before swallowing. "Is it cinnamon?" he asked.

"Something very like, fermented with honey over several years."

"Years?" He regarded the flask with suspicion. "Must

be expensive."

"It was, so enjoy it."

Scarlet drank again and shook the wind-blown hair out of his eyes.

"I have a surprise for you," Liall said. Scarlet's eyebrows crept up. "Shall we go see?"

Scarlet shrugged and took a last sip from the flask. Liall capped it and slipped it back inside his shirt.

Once they were in the cabin, Liall closed the door and locked it before stripping off his gloves.

Scarlet looked pointedly at the lock, but said nothing. When he saw what Liall had commanded the crew to bring in while they were gone, he laughed out loud. "A bath?" Scarlet gave a startled laugh. "That can't be fresh water."

"It is," Liall said. "Well, not really. It is melted ice from the floes. It has some salt in it, but not much. It is perfectly fine for bathing, though I would not drink it if I were you." He threw a few more coals onto the small brazier and opened the vents up a little. They all froze on the voyage, but he knew Scarlet felt it more than any other. Rshani mariners were accustomed to such weather and thought nothing of it. Liall had overheard the crude comments that floated around the ship regarding the Hilurin's constant need for warmth as well as his habit of washing, which the rough mariners thought faintly womanish, but Liall did not have to share a cabin with the mariners. If Scarlet intended to smell sweet throughout the voyage, he would get no argument from Liall.

Scarlet trailed his fingers through the steaming water in the copper tub. It was an oval tub without feet, and had a thick wooden rim. There was a crescent moon sliver of hard, brown soap resting on the floor near the tub. "I haven't had a real bath since we left Volkovoi."

"I know."

"Very funny. You're no rose, yourself."

"I am so. I bathed earlier in the captain's quarters." Liall sat on the bunk and leaned back on his elbows. "Well?"

Scarlet ducked his head. Liall thought it was so that the blush that rose to the pedlar's cheeks would be hidden from him, but Scarlet met his eyes boldly a moment later.

"You must think I'm very silly. Isn't that what your Kasiri say about my people?" Scarlet tilted his head and delivered a fair imitation of Peysho's coarse speech: "Puffed-up little Hilurin prigs, all of 'em. Now't the brains to come in out th' rain."

Liall smiled. "I confess. At first, I thought of you as a prim little Hilurin with too much pride and not enough sense, but I have not had that thought in a long time. I have nothing but respect for you, Scarlet. You are more of a man than many warriors."

Scarlet seemed to consider for a moment, then nodded as if he had made up his mind. Holding Liall's gaze steadily, he unbuckled the overcoat and tossed it to the bunk. The red leather jacket was next, and then he tugged the hem of the rough linen shirt from the waistband of his breeches and pulled it over his head. He stopped then and looked at Liall with a strange sort of intensity, as if wondering who he was.

Liall stared. By the Shining Ones, but he was lovely! Scarlet's ivory skin was like fresh cream, unmarked and hairless except for a fine dusting that arrowed down from his indented navel and vanished into his breeches. His chest and upper arms were finely-sculpted – not brawny but certainly no weakling – and his narrow waist was flat and hard. He found himself staring at Scarlet's slender collarbones, fascinated by the shadings of delicate color in their hollows, pearl and pale rose on white, and fascinated also by the small peaks of his nipples below, pale and pink as a blush.

Scarlet crossed his arms over his chest. "Am I..." he trailed off. Scarlet's black hair had grown shaggy in the past month, and the cut under his right eye had closed to a thick red line that would leave a permanent scar. He brushed the hair out of his eyes and tried again, shyly: "Do I please you?"

Liall shook his head. For a moment, a crestfallen look stole over Scarlet's features. "Scarlet," Liall said. His own voice sounded very odd to him, tight and hoarse as it was. He judged it a sign of nerves. "You are most pleasing. How can you not know how you look?"

The light was back in Scarlet's eyes. He shrugged. "I'm all right, I guess. Never had any complaints." That last bit might have sounded like boasting, and Scarlet cleared his throat and looked embarrassed. "Not that there's been anyone who'd have a right to." He sat on the bunk to strip off his boots, and then quickly unbuckled his belt and began to slide his breeches off his hips as he sat. He blushed and his hands faltered as the high color again flooded his cheeks.

"Please continue," Liall said. He was fast becoming enamored of that blush; the way it spread across Scarlet's face and chin and even the bridge of his nose when he was the least embarrassed or frightened or angry. It was such a charming trait, so without artifice or pretense, and even though Liall knew it only happened when Scarlet was distressed, he could not make himself fall out of love with it. Rshani did not blush very easily, if at all. Apart from anything else, they did not have the color for it.

Liall thought Scarlet might demur after all and back out of whatever he had been considering, but with a long, searching look, Scarlet skinned the breeches down his legs and kicked them off.

Liall inhaled shakily: uncomplicated as ever, Scarlet wore nothing underneath. Below Scarlet's hips, the line of fine hairs that plunged down from his navel briefly spread out into a soft-looking triangle of dark hair. There was very little hair near his sex, and between his thighs there seemed to be none. Liall wondered for a moment if Scarlet shaved there, then remembered his few experiences with Hilurin girls, and how their pubic hairs had been like sea foam and nearly invisible, and how they seemed to have no other hair at all on their bodies.

Red-faced, Scarlet moved to get into the short tub.

"Wait," Liall begged.

Scarlet hesitated, and Liall saw a brief flash of fear in his eyes.

Liall longed to gather Scarlet in his arms and soothe those cares, but he was afraid to move and break whatever fragile spell was holding them in place.

"Turn around," Liall asked. "Please."

Scarlet inhaled and seemed to be wrestling with some inner demon, but he turned slowly on his heel, giving Liall an unspoiled view of his back. Liall saw with a flash of relief that Scarlet's shoulders and lower back were no longer mottled with bruises. His eyes lingered on the legs and the round, full curve of Scarlet's bottom before Scarlet turned to face him again. Liall's gaze dropped, and he saw that Scarlet was not totally unmoved.

The water rippled and splashed onto the floor as Scarlet climbed into the tub quickly. Scarlet took up the sliver of hard soap and began to lather it in his hands, spreading the slick stuff over his arms and shoulders and throat, as Liall fought for control. The soap exuded a smell rather like cloves, the scent filling the cabin.

By the gods, Liall thought suddenly, it is a good thing he has no inkling of the power he holds over me!

They will see it in Rshan, the dark half of his mind

whispered to him. He will be a liability there. They will use him, and through him, you.

Well, they could try. He had been used before and knew what it felt like. Vigilance would be his armor. He would just have to guard Scarlet closely and persuade the young man to follow his lead.

That will work splendidly, he thought, seeing as how obedient Scarlet has been up until now.

Liall snorted. Scarlet glanced at him.

"Something wrong?"

"Only thinking,"

"Oh." Scarlet continued to work the soap into his skin, paying close attention to his hands and the dirt ground under his fingernails. Then he ducked his head under the water and scrubbed soap through his hair, washing away the inevitable grime of shipboard life. Last, he did his feet, folding his knees up awkwardly, one by one, and bracing them on the iron lip as he scrubbed the lather vigorously between his toes.

"You have nice feet," Liall observed. He did, white and pink and narrow, with a high arch and round little toenails, neatly trimmed. Scarlet grinned at the odd compliment. Water sloshed over the side as he moved the soap over his chest, rubbing lower across his belly. Again, Liall's throat grew tight.

Liall got up and knelt beside the tub, not caring that he was getting the knees of his breeches wet. "Shall I scrub your back?"

Scarlet handed over the soap with a trembling hand. He leaned forward in the water, averting his eyes and clasping his hands together under the water. Liall stroked the slippery crescent across Scarlet's back, his dark fingers kneading into white skin, easing the knots he found there. Scarlet's head tipped back instinctively and he gave a little purring noise of enjoyment.

Liall felt himself beginning to grow taut and hard between his legs. Laced through his excitement was a tendril of fear. He could almost deal more easily with the fear. This was dangerous, for he had already had it proven to him, in the plainest of terms, that he was quite susceptible to being overwhelmed by sensation when it came to Scarlet. He had committed more unwise acts in the past two months than he had in the ten years previous. Scarlet clouded his senses, tainted everything with an aura of eroticism, just by being near him. Liall wanted him desperately, wanted to lie with him, be inside of him, taste Scarlet's mouth and skin as Scarlet came helplessly for him, crying out his name.

The soap slipped from Liall's grasp and vanished in the water. Too late, Liall realized that his hands had roamed to Scarlet's chest, and that he was caressing more than he was washing. Scarlet turned his head.

Liall gazed into Scarlet's incredibly dark eyes. They were wide and black, and his lips were parted in fear or passion. They were both slightly out of breath, Liall still frozen, Scarlet trembling on the verge of action.

"Liall?"

Liall moved his hand to the back of Scarlet's neck, and he moved his fingers through the wet strands there, the sensation grounding him into the present. But Scarlet seemed to need him to say something, to give some sign.

"What is it?"

Scarlet searched Liall's pale eyes, and then slowly scanned the lines of Liall's face, taking in the shapes of the man as if he could learn Liall like a lesson to heart. Finally, his gaze returned to Liall's eyes, and he gave a thin, sad smile. The water rippled as Scarlet lifted his shoulders in a small shrug.

"I love you, Liall."

The confession caught Liall completely unprepared.

He had never had those particular words handed to him in such a self deprecating way, as if Scarlet was offering him a poor gift and had to apologize for the lack. Liall licked his lips before speaking.

"Since I came to the Southern Continent I have only had whores, mercenary soldiers, and bhoros boys. I do not know how to behave with someone like you."

"Like me?"

"A man with honor."

Scarlet's expression flickered. His smile grew warmer, and he lifted his hand out of the water and cupped Liall's face. "I won't be offended if you touch me, you stupid Kasiri bastard. I want you to."

Liall's breath caught and he gave a weak sounding moan and pulled Scarlet to him, covering that beautiful mouth with his own, framing Scarlet's face between his wet hands and kissing the younger man hungrily. His tongue sought entrance between Scarlet's lips and he moaned again and stroked inside the pedlar's mouth sweetly. He needed Scarlet to understand, and words were such a barrier. Liall tried to communicate what he felt, striving to transfer to Scarlet, by touch of tongue and teeth and lips, how much his love was returned.

They were both shaking when Liall drew back. "T'aishka," Liall gasped, daring to take another kiss, to suck the wet, lush, lower lip gently into his mouth. He moaned and flicked his tongue against Scarlet's, driving into the heat of that lovely mouth. Liall wanted to pull Scarlet out of the water and throw him onto the bunk, cover his naked body with kisses and drown in him, but he was afraid to. So very afraid. They were both too shadowed, too full of fear and distrust and echoes of things neither of them would name.

Whose fear? Liall asked himself. Is it really Scarlet you are trying to protect?

Scarlet's hands touched Liall's face, learning every curve and ridge. "Teach me how to say that."

Liall shook his head, but he said it anyway. "T'aishka."

Scarlet tried, mangling it. Liall smothered the word under another kiss and his hands went under Scarlet's arms, lifting. Scarlet stood up, dripping and dazed, and — Liall saw plainly — very much affected by the kiss. Liall grabbed an Rshani-sized towel from the bunk and wrapped Scarlet into it. It engulfed his small frame like a blanket.

Liall steered him toward the bunk. "Get under the covers quickly," Liall advised. The cabin was still very chilly.

Scarlet scrubbed his wet hair with the towel and climbed into the bunk. Liall rubbed a shaky hand over his face and glanced to the door. He seriously considered fleeing.

Scarlet moved part of the thick covers aside and looked up at Liall. "I'd be warmer with you beside me."

He is so beautiful, Liall thought, unspoiled and almost painfully young, flushed with drink and clean desire, and wanting me. He does want me.

Liall's last reserve of resistance crumbled, and he climbed carefully into the bunk.

Scarlet's glance was mischievous. "This is hardly fair. You're still wearing all your clothes."

"Not for long," Liall said roughly. He tugged his shirt up over his head and tossed it aside. Now he could feel Scarlet's skin against his own, and he moaned at the shock that raced through his body, like static in the air on a cold, dry day. Shifting his knees onto the bed, Liall prowled over Scarlet's body. He kept them apart, over him but not touching him, supporting himself on his arms, his entire body drawn tight with tension, his nerves flitting like a hummingbird. He thought he saw a shadow of fear in Scarlet's face for a moment.

"Only touching," Liall promised.

Scarlet tried not to look relieved, but Liall was watching him too closely. He saw it in the way Scarlet's shoulders lost that squared set and his back settled against the mattress, the way his knees moved apart willingly as Liall carefully settled down to lie upon him. Liall supported some of his weight on his elbows and was careful not to let his belt buckle scratch Scarlet's skin.

Scarlet shivered a little, either from cold or excitement.

"Are you cold again?" Liall whispered, brushing Scarlet's lips with his own. "I shall warm you." That lavish mouth the color of rose petals, so sinful a mouth, yet he tasted like innocence and clean water. Liall kissed him deeply, sealing their mouths together as the waves sighed and rolled. Scarlet melted into it, his arms winding around Liall's neck, holding on as Liall kissed him long and thoroughly. When they finally drew apart, Scarlet was shaking.

"Is this...?" Liall could not finish the thought.

Scarlet nodded, quick and breathless, and sought Liall's mouth again. Scarlet's lips were parted and eager, and Liall pressed forward with his tongue, luxuriating in the feel of being close at last. Scarlet was here with him, and there was no anger or insults between them, no fear or shying away from the truth. Liall slipped his hand between their bodies and grasped stretched, silken flesh.

Scarlet gasped. His hips pushed up to meet Liall's hand, and he began to make small noises in his throat, sucking eagerly on Liall's tongue.

Liall very gently eased his hand away and began to undo his belt and the line of buttons at the front of his breeches. Scarlet tried to pull back a little to see what he was doing.

"Only touching," Liall reassured in a whisper as he flicked aside the last button and freed his cock, which was already hard and aching. Scarlet could surely feel him, even if he could not see, and the pedlar gave a low, shuddering moan as Liall wrapped his hand around both of their members, stretching his fingers to fit, and began to stroke them off together.

Something was expanding in Liall's chest, a hollow space that was being filled with the scent of sun-warmed skin and shining black hair, eyes dark as jet yet never cold: a red-hooded pedlar with the pride and fire of a king, a boy with the courage of a man.

"I love you," Liall gasped in Scarlet's ear, his mouth to Scarlet's cheek. "Oh, gods, I love you!"

Scarlet's hands gripped Liall's shoulders hard just before the younger man shuddered violently and came hotly over Liall's fingers with a startled shout, his release spilling over and slicking Liall's hand. Scarlet's seed eased the way for Liall and he moved his hand faster, harder. For the first time in years, Liall spent in less than a minute, crying out loudly as his hips jerked and he striped Scarlet's belly with his release.

After a while, the world righted itself again, and Liall looked down to see Scarlet staring at him with wide, astonished eyes.

"What?" Liall whispered. He reached up and traced wet fingers over Scarlet's mouth. He felt as tender now as he had fierce a moment earlier. This one had his heart, no doubting it. He wondered if Scarlet truly knew how much that frightened him, how much the warm ache in his chest made him want to run from Scarlet as if the young man were a demon after his soul.

"I didn't..." Scarlet's throat moved as he swallowed and blinked. "I didn't know it would be like this."

For a moment, Liall was terrified. He began to lift himself up.

"No," Scarlet said quickly, his arms going around Liall's back. "Stay. I just..." he took a deep breath. "I don't have the words, Liall. I don't know how to say what you make me feel."

Liall kissed him softly, touched but fearful yet. "But I pleased you?"

Scarlet's grin was genuine and a little sheepish. "Oh, yes. A lot. You?"

"You may as well ask me if I like to breathe air." Scarlet's brows drew together, puzzling that out for a moment. Liall poked him in the ribs. "Don't be a ninny," he said, borrowing one of Scarlet's phrases. "I loved it. I love you." His head was still swimming. Dangerous. Oh, it was dangerous. "I love you. Right now, I love just about everything."

They laughed and they kissed, and later Liall pleasured Scarlet again with his hand and showed him what more there was to loving, touching his tongue to Scarlet's nipples as the young man strained and thrust up into his fist. Scarlet insisted on undressing Liall fully and doing the same for him, more slowly this time. Scarlet's young face was very serious and intent as he studied Liall's reactions and stroked and learned the golden-hued, powerful body, pressing kisses to Liall's mouth and throat until Liall was lost in the sweetness of it, still frightened of the warm feeling in his chest. They fell asleep wrapped around each other, the creaking of timbers and the flutter of the candle flame lulling worry to rest and their minds to sleep.

Liall woke in the night and listened to the sea and the sounds of the ship. Scarlet was warm against him, and he remembered what had happened between them, the things that were said and the promise that their bodies had made.

What was I thinking of?

You were thinking of a life before this one, he told himself. Of two lives, actually: one where you lived in Rshan as an honorable man, and another where you were a lawless Kasiri bandit in Byzantur. Neither life was particularly worth living. This new life — this new beginning — will be with Scarlet, and this time, you will not fail. You will not be arriving in Rshan the same numbed and shattered man who left those shores. You will not be Liall the Wolf, either.

Who will I be?

He drowsed with that question circling his mind like a shark in dangerous waters.

Nine days later, sailing on a fair sea through a blue, frozen dawn, the quartermaster sighted land. They had arrived in Rshan na Ostre.

7.

The Land of Night

The day they sailed into port was a twilight day, as the last few weeks had been, and snowing heavily. Scarlet hardly noticed, he was so amazed by the city.

It's just like something out of the ancient tales, he thought. This really is Rshan, and people actually live here. Amazing!

It was a city coiled like a white dragon on the edges of the harbor, woven of magic and blue flame, with scales of snow and fangs of ice, narrow streets winding like a serpent's tail, and tall, carved buildings thrusting up like horns, with towers and misty spires in the distance. A sapphire-blue glow seemed to hover over both the harbor and the city beyond.

Scarlet stood beside Liall and stared, his jaw hanging open. "Is it real?" he asked stupidly.

"Too real for me," Liall said. His fingers brushed down Scarlet's arm.

Scarlet leaned into him, liking the touch, but Liall sounded sad.

"What's this place called?"

"Nau Karmun," Liall said. His tone was strange.

"Is this your home?" Scarlet ventured further.

"Yes. And no," Liall answered. "This is the realm of Kalas Nauhin, the South Kingdom. Here there are the great and elegant cities of Rshan and the court of

Camira Druz. Further north – much further – beyond the mountain range is Fanorl Nauhin, the North Kingdom, and in that place there are only wild tribes and savage places without names."

Scarlet was astonished. Not one but two Rshani peoples! "Are they your enemies?" he asked, his interest greatly piqued.

Liall smiled a little. "Not as a Byzan would recognize an enemy. There has been war between us, and we have killed one another, yet we are bound together. There is much between us that cannot be laid to rest."

The ship dropped anchor and a number of skiffs left the wharf and began moving across the water toward them. Liall watched silently for a while before looking down at Scarlet.

"Do you see the great stone gate there, just beyond that line of buildings? That is the entrance to the city proper. That is where we will go." His hand tightened on Scarlet's arm. "It is where I will, again, pledge my word for you."

"Oh," Scarlet said, but he thought: Now what?

Liall discerned his anxiety. "No, t'aishka. This time you will be treated with respect. I swear it."

Scarlet wondered if that were possible. He bit his lip and leaned into the gunwale until the first of the skiffs reached the ship. Liall took some minutes to bid farewell to Captain Qixa. They spoke back and forth in Sinha, and Liall's voice was low and soft. He took off his glove and clasped arms with Qixa, and the bald captain beamed and bowed, very gratified. They parted and Qixa even spared a pleasant nod for Scarlet.

He's probably just glad to see me go, Scarlet thought. The quartermaster's eye caught his, and Scarlet nodded shortly.

"You made it, lenilyn!" the quartermaster called out,

and then showed him his yellowed teeth in a bellowing laugh.

"What's so funny?"

The mariner shook his head, laughing. "You were good luck for me, Byzan child. I made many coins betting on you. No one thought you would reach our shores alive!"

Scarlet shook his head and laughed with him. "Let that be a lesson to you, then!"

The quartermaster gave a cocky salute as Liall descended the rope ladder into the skiff, and then it was Scarlet's turn. Climbing down was tricky stuff. The rope ladder swayed sickeningly with the motion of the brigantine, and the skiff seemed to be much further away now that he was over the side. He stopped and held on for a moment, his arms shaking with strain, before resuming his descent. Liall took hold of him when he was near the bottom, steadying him as he stepped off into the skiff.

Liall winked. "You're almost a proper mariner now, little Byzan," he said lowly.

"I'm not—"

"Little," Liall finished. "I know."

Scarlet decided Liall was patronizing him, and he gave the man a cross look as he sat on the wooden seat of the skiff, holding on grimly. Although he had long ago lost any trace of his former seasickness, he would never really feel at home on the water. To Scarlet, water travel was something that just had to be endured in order to get from one place to another. He would never love it as Liall did.

Liall patted Scarlet's knee before falling silent, and the skiff began to scull away from the hull of the brigantine, the oarsmen pulling with strong strokes and chanting in time.

Scarlet reached out and touched the smooth, cold wood of the Ostre Sul, giving a silent thanks to the vessel for carrying him so far from home and bringing him safe to shore. He also spared a prayer for Deva, which he had forgotten to do for days now, and as he was looking up to the sky, he caught a last glimpse of Oleksei's stony face before the water bore them away. Shivering in the cold, Scarlet added a prayer that he would never see that particular Rshani ever again.

The wind off the water was bitter, even with the woolen cap and the heavy coat Liall had given him to wear over his red jacket. The dark-faced oarsmen chanted in Sinha as they rocked and bumped their way into the harbor. The skiff crew looked at him now and then with curious eyes. No hostility, which was a welcome change.

Liall grew tenser as they neared the wharf, and his arm went around Scarlet and tightened like steel. Scarlet squirmed a little when it became uncomfortable, and Liall started, as if he had forgotten Scarlet was there. Scarlet put his gloved hand in Liall's, reckoning that the atya was facing old demons here.

"T'aishka," Liall murmured and tangled his long fingers with Scarlet's briefly before moving his hand away. Liall did not speak again until after they arrived on solid ground and began walking through the crowded pier.

"Keep close," Liall murmured with a warning glance.

"Do not say a word."

They navigated the crowds of workers and mariners, their heads down, speaking to no one, but there were stares. A younger mariner clad in fur and leather pointed at Scarlet and said something rather loud. Heads turned. Someone pointed to Scarlet's dark hair and quite clearly said the word *lenilyn*, provoking more stares and comments, and then Liall was thrusting Scarlet behind their escort with a curse and pulling his cap down tighter over his black hair.

Scarlet was shivering nonstop when they arrived at a

great stone gate, which led into an enormous corridor, lined with guards. Liall paused in front of it, hesitating, then set his jaw and led the way inside.

As they walked along the wide path with its foreign traceries set into the stone, Scarlet found himself wondering what it must be like for Liall, coming home again after so long, being unsure of his welcome or even his safety, and what was so dreadful that Liall would not even speak of it. Scarlet was not sure how long Liall had been away from Rshan, only that Liall was not so very much older than him, so it could not have been more than ten years or so.

There's so much I don't know about him, he thought. And not for lack of asking. Why does he guard his past so closely, and what is he afraid of?

Some way into the corridor, they came to a group of soldiers dressed in warm wool with fur ruffs around their collars, much like the one Scarlet had first seen Liall wearing at the Kasiri camp. They were very well-armed.

Liall seemed to grow even taller. He took off his right glove, and Scarlet saw the glimmer of silver in the torchlight. It was a ring made of silver and sapphire, one that Scarlet had not seen Liall wear before. Liall held his right hand out to the hard-faced soldier who approached him, speaking in commanding tones, words that Scarlet did not understand either in sense or intonation. He wondered where the ring had come from and why Liall had kept it hidden. Scarlet watched as the soldier's stolid expression changed to one of uncertainty and shocked respect. The soldier bowed his head to Liall.

Scaja was right, Scarlet thought in awe, not only well-born, but well-known. Liall's family name must carry a lot of weight here. That must be what the ring is for.

The astonished soldier stepped back and another, younger man pushed forward. He was not dressed like the soldiers, but wore fine robes of blue accented with silver, and some kind of sunburst badge or medallion of office on his shoulder. He had a kind face and handsome features, evident even through his surprise.

"Jochi," Liall said with perfect calm.

The young man went to one knee and bowed low before speaking rapidly and intently.

Liall acknowledged the kneeling man's words with a single, curt nod of his head. "Come, Scarlet," he said in Bizye, his words a cloak of quiet dignity. "Transport awaits us."

On his feet again, the man Liall had addressed as Jochi gave Scarlet a startled glace and looked like he was going to make trouble. Scarlet heard the word *lenilyn* again and there was a surge of hostility from the soldiers surrounding them. Liall said something sharp, his voice like the lash of a whip, and got another bow from the soldiers before Jochi led them through the rest of the corridor. They stepped out into the snowy twilight again, but the wind was less. That was a great relief to Scarlet, whose feet and hands were quite numb. The healing scar on his cheek throbbed with the cold.

Their transport was a strange contraption, like a child's sled, only much larger and with a body like Scarlet had seen on carriages in the capital of Byzantur. This one had real glass in the carriage windows, not shutters, and it was all agleam with polished black wood and bright brass runners.

"What is it?" he asked Liall quietly, thinking how much Scaja would have liked to have seen this thing. Being the son of a wainwright, he was no less awed than Scaja would have been. Scarlet wanted to share this with Liall, but the man was far away, his expression distant.

"It is called a sleigh."

"Slain?" Scarlet ventured, but Liall shook his head

with annoyance.

One of the tall soldiers opened the door to the carriage and bowed. Liall nudged Scarlet's shoulder, indicating that he should go first, ignoring the surprise on the soldier's face.

The interior was luxurious with furs and cushions piled high on a sort of bed or couch against the rear housing. The door closed and the sleigh began to move forward. Now that they were alone, Liall drew Scarlet close to his side and began to pull the furs over them both.

"We have a long way to ride," Liall explained softly. He rubbed Scarlet's arms, and then took his other glove off to touch Scarlet's face. "You are so cold."

"Where are we going?"

Liall ignored the question and rubbed Scarlet's hands through the gloves. "How do your toes feel?"

"Numb," he confessed. "Stop fretting."

Liall frowned, but obeyed. Between body heat and the furs, Scarlet was soon much warmer. He did not recognize what kind of beast the furs might be taken from, but they were silky soft and obviously costly. Some were black and some were of a bluish gray that he had never seen before, and very large. He could not imagine the animal it had once graced. "Where are we going?" Scarlet asked again.

"To my home."

That was not informative, but again, Scarlet reckoned with Liall's demons and began to poke around the inside of the carriage. There was a door on either side of the contraption, and he leaned forward and peered through the little window on his side. It looked like they were passing tenements and warehouses, very like to what one would see in the port of Ankar, but sturdier and much cleaner. Huddled figures stood bunched around small fires near the waterline, their hands held out for warmth.

Workers, no doubt.

The sleigh was moving with astonishing speed, far faster than any cart Scarlet had ever ridden in. It jolted suddenly and he drew back from the window with a hiss.

"Do not be afraid," Liall said, and for a moment he was back all the way, his eyes focused on the present, not looking into whatever memories possessed him. "It was a bump in the snow. We shall not overturn, these are balanced well."

"I'm not afraid," Scarlet said with dignity, which was partly true, "Only startled. We're moving so fast!"

Liall nodded and sank back into his thoughts. He ignored Scarlet after that, and Scarlet settled into the far side of the seat and looked out the window. They had moved past the tenements and into an area of small shops crowded together in tall buildings. He watched and noticed that everyone went heavily dressed in woolen coats and boots and none neglected to wear some manner of hat or head covering. He stared at the conical fur hats that most of the people wore. They had long flaps to cover the ears and odd little flaps on the top, which folded down and were decorated with many kinds of stitching and beads. Mostly, Scarlet was amazed at the lights: torches, lamps and candlelight were everywhere, a glittering city of light. He wondered at his surprise. Obviously, the winter darkness would necessitate the need for light even in the hours that were marked as day, but these folk seemed to love light and revel in it. He saw that in the way they decorated their lamps with colored bits of glass and dressed up their street lanterns with wrought iron and cut crystal and panels of painted paper. Scarlet had a hundred questions about the city, but Liall brooded silently on his side of the couch and Scarlet did not want to risk treading on whatever was haunting him.

They traveled so quickly, it seemed hardly any time at all until they were in a wealthy part of the city. Sleighs passed them on the road, some open and plain, with men and women bundled in wool and sheepskin. But most of the sleighs were closed, the exteriors richly painted and decorated. They left the city soon after that, and the heavy traffic gave way to almost none as they moved into the countryside surrounding the port and began to pass great mansions fairly glowing with light, and surrounded by snowy expanses.

Scarlet could not see what lay before them on the roadway, but after a time, he noticed that nothing but snow and trees filled the landscape. And such trees! No plain brown or black trunks here, but pale like the petals of white roses, or Linhona's clean linens. The tall, slender trees, barren of leaves, were all of a ghostly white color, whip-stroked here and there with black. They were nothing like the weather-blasted junipers and pines he was familiar with in Byzantur, and the lack of familiar plants just seemed to highlight how alien this land was, and how alien he was in it.

Scarlet turned to Liall to ask him about the trees, but he seemed to be dozing, his eyes closed and his arms crossed over his chest. It occurred to Scarlet that he might try to do the same, not knowing what awaited them or how much energy he would need, but the landscape, the new sights and smells, fascinated him so. Despite all that, in less than an hour he was fighting to keep his eyes open. The movement of the sleigh lulled him until it finally won and he slept.

Scarlet woke with a start some time later and found he was lying curled on the wide seat under a layer of furs, his cheek against Liall's shoulder. Liall was peering out the window. "We are nearly there," he said without looking at Scarlet.

"Liall?"

Liall gave Scarlet an unconvincing smile. "What is wrong?"

Scarlet hesitated. "Nothing," he said finally.

Liall sighed. "Do you remember when we sparred on the deck of the *Ostre Sul?* It is like that with me now. I am only remembering. It happens to the best of soldiers."

Scarlet was not reassured.

"Please do not worry," Liall said. "Whatever comes, I am with you."

Scarlet squeezed Liall's hand, his heart going out to the man. "Don't vex yourself on my account. I'll be fine, like always. Just do what you have to do."

Liall nodded absently.

The sleigh turned sharply, and Scarlet gasped at the new vista beyond the window. He had thought the city was beautiful, but the castle fortress before him was ten times that. Blue light from lanterns of the same color, lights and spires and towers, all laced with icicles and snow, beautiful carved domes of blue and silver, and battlements that seemed to reach into the very sky, all twinkling with that luminous blue light.

"My home," Liall said. "The Nauhinir."

Scarlet stared, his mouth dry. Before he could summon the wits to mouth the questions drumming in his brain, the sleigh began to slow.

"Take off that coat," Liall said, meaning the heavy overcoat he had found for Scarlet on the ship, now frayed and white-patched with salt. Scarlet removed it, keeping only his red pedlar's coat on, which was also travel-worn but still better than the coat. The crimson color was fading from exposure to the salt air, but it was still deep and brilliant.

"And the cap, and your weapons," Liall added, drawing off his own coat and pulling a long cloak from his pack. It was deep blue with some sort of curling silver design splashed over it in long slashes. It looked very fine. Scarlet wondered where he had gotten such a cloak. Such a garment would have spoiled fast at sea if Liall had worn it on the ship.

Scarlet removed his Morturii knives from his belt with misgiving, pulled his cap off and tried to comb his tangled hair with his fingers. It had grown longer on the voyage. "Where'd you get that cloak? It's grand."

Liall did not answer, and before he could ask again, the sleigh came to an abrupt stop and the door opened.

Liall rose and stepped out, whipping the blue cloak around his body, and then turned to hold out his hand for Scarlet. It seemed an odd thing to do, helping him out of the carriage as if he were a lady or invalid, but he was in Liall's land now. For all he knew, this was a proper custom. It was not until they were standing in the snow under the blue lamplight that Scarlet saw there were men and women outside the great fortress, waiting for them on the wide steps of a stone gatehouse that was larger than the army barracks in Patra. Everyone here was taller than him by yards and yards, it seemed.

"What is this place?" Scarlet whispered.

"The Nauhinir, as I have said," Liall answered tightly out of the side of his mouth, which told him nothing more than a name.

The people were dressed in furs and bright fabrics, as if they could deny the bleak landscape simply by the colors they adorned themselves in. Brilliant jewels glittered on the ears and throats of both men and women, and many wore the same kind of comical fur hat Scarlet had seen in the city, though richer and more heavily decorated. He stared at the broad stone steps that led upward, intimidated by the sheer size of everything, and the men and women surrounding him were like pillars of gold, tall and unapproachable. He smoothed his hands down his red jacket, knowing that his boots and shirt were mended and he looked poor and uncouth beside Liall.

Liall took his arm. "Now I must ask you to remain silent until we are alone together. If I nod at you, deliver your best bow."

Scarlet nodded, painfully aware of the many pale eyes on him. Never more keenly had he felt the differences between him and Liall. Liall turned to the men who waited. They bowed to him. Liall did not bow back, but kept hold of Scarlet's arm as he guided him up the stone steps that were so deep that Scarlet's legs ached by the time they reached the top.

Two enormous iron doors – gates, really – opened inward, pulled by several men in blue and silver livery. Scarlet wondered briefly if they were servants or soldiers as Liall swept him in, past the great gates and past glittering folk in silks and heavy velvets and furs, into the largest hall Scarlet had ever seen. The gates closed behind them with a muffled, booming noise that rang throughout the hall like muted thunder, and Scarlet thought that this place must hold great treasures indeed, for surely not even an army could breach those gates.

Liall continued to lead them forward. Scarlet had to practically bite his tongue to prevent more questions from falling out, but he decided that to mimic Liall was probably the best course of action. From the edge of his vision, he could see everyone bowing low, men and women alike, but Liall strode with his head high and his eyes forward, not returning the proffered respect. Suddenly, though he had always been at ease around strangers and new surroundings, Scarlet was frozen into some inner stillness and fear. There was something here that he did not understand.

A man dressed as richly as the rest approached and bowed low. Liall spoke to him clearly and loudly. The man flicked a glance at Scarlet, and Scarlet immediately sensed danger. The man spoke a few words in the rapid Sinha dialect, and Scarlet looked up at Liall.

"He is only greeting me," Liall explained. His dislike of the strange man was plain.

"Who's Nazheer. Nazur..." Scarlet's tongue tripped on the unfamiliar sounds. "What he said?"

"Nazheradei," Liall supplied. "It is me, it is my name. Prince Nazheradei. Now be silent."

Scarlet stared at him, frozen in that odd stillness. He heard nothing but a rushing sound in his ears, felt nothing but the cold.

Liall led him forward again and Scarlet allowed it, moving woodenly. A set of tall, carved doors opened and they entered together.

Dozens of delicate lamps made of gilt and glass hung from chains suspended from the ceiling, scattering golden light on the walls, which were covered with large panels of polished, inlaid woods. An older woman with pure white hair sat at the far end of the high-ceilinged, opulent room, jewels glittering at her throat, her gown like a cobweb of silver. She wore a circlet of clear crystals – surely they couldn't be diamonds! – binding her brow. Though she was a woman and much older, the angular shape of her face was very much like Liall's, and Scarlet realized with a shock who she must be.

A crown, he thought numbly, and stopped when Liall stopped. Behind the crowned woman was another, younger, woman: the coldest, most beautiful woman Scarlet had ever seen, with pale gold hair and eyes like chips of ice. Her name, Scarlet learned later, was Shikhoza.

His gypsy chief was a prince. The prince and the pedlar. If Scarlet could have made any sound at all, he would have barked laughter like a madman.

8.

Nazheradei

Liall pointedly did not place his foot on the lowest step of the dais, claiming a prince's status, but instead stayed on the main platform, watching and waiting.

"Welcome home, my son."

"I thank you, my mother."

There were no courtly speeches. Rshan greetings are swift and to the point. This saved time for later, when Rshani are disposed to better carving each other up. At Liall's side, Scarlet had gone deathly still, and he gripped Liall hand tightly, as if afraid he might be eaten by all these giants. Liall drew him forward and presented him to Queen Nadiushka.

"This is Scarlet of Lysia."

Her silvery eyebrows under her diamond crown rose slightly.

"My t'aishka," Liall finished, and her eyebrows went higher still. Liall nudged Scarlet with his elbow. The pedlar jumped and looked at Liall with round, frightened eyes.

"Bow," Liall muttered, knowing the boy had forgotten. Scarlet could hardly be blamed for that. A surge of guilt nudged his conscience.

Scarlet took a deep breath and looked up at the mistress of the Nauhinir Palace, the Queen of Rshan na Ostre, then put his hand over his heart and sketched a brief, old-fashioned bow.

Liall glanced to Nadiushka and saw the corners of her eyes crinkle with amusement. When had she acquired those wrinkles? Ai, my mother, despite your vow, you have grown old after all.

The amusement that rippled through the glittering court was less kind, for Scarlet's greeting was far less than should be rendered to a Queen, but Scarlet was oblivious to all of it.

Liall, however, was not. He lifted the edge of his cloak and draped it over Scarlet's shoulders along with his arm, then pulled the Hilurin closer to his side. Now there would be no mistakes, since he had publicly claimed Scarlet. Liall could feel his trembling through the cloak, though he hid it well enough.

Then his mother did something that surprised Liall. She rose from her throne and descended the three steps down to where they stood. She looked at Liall for a long moment, and from this distance there was no mistaking her age. No amount of powder or jewels could hide the deep lines around her mouth and the dull, gray strands threaded carefully through her hair. Rshani do not age in quite the same way as the other races, but she had grown elderly in his absence. He saw it in her skin and in her hands and most of all in the tears that glimmered in her pale blue eyes, so like his own. *And Nadei's*, a silken voice seemed to hiss in Liall's mind.

She put her hands on Liall's shoulders and placed a kiss in the center of his forehead: an extraordinary greeting from a Queen. Liall thought nothing she could do now would astonish him further, but then she turned to Scarlet and kissed him in the same manner, and he, knowing no better, briefly touched her arm in return. She was not offended, though well she might have been once. Liall, too, had a prickly sense of pride, and he had learned it from his mother. Liall had never known King Lindolanen, his father, for the young king had had been killed hunting a snow bear while Nadei was still toddling. Nadiushka had been pregnant with Liall that year, and he had been born to a widowed mother, a matter thought to be an ill-omened thing in Rshan.

Well, Liall thought, they had not been wrong.

She turned and motioned, and from behind the throne came a sturdy boy of fourteen or so with a look of her about his mouth and eyes. Liall had had no reliable news from Rshan in ages, but he could guess who the boy was. He was tall, handsome, but not overly so, and he looked at Liall with wariness and more than a little suspicion. Liall found a moment to be desperately thankful that the boy resembled Nadei not at all.

"Cestimir," the Queen called, drawing him to her. He was almost as tall as she. "This is your elder brother, Nazheradei." She smoothed Cestimir's hair, which was like silver silk and curling at the ends. "This is Cestimir, my son."

No bows were necessary between them, blood prince to crown prince, being from the same wellspring, but Liall sensed deep currents flowing around the court. There was anger here, which was nothing new, but also a sense of urgency that he had not felt since...

Don't think about that day. Not now. Not here.

Led by instinct alone, Liall touched his forehead and bowed low, nudging Scarlet to follow his lead. Scarlet did, and when Liall lifted his gaze, he saw the suspicion fade from Cestimir's eyes. Too quickly, for a courtly bow costs nothing and means nothing. It made him suddenly afraid for him, and for his mother.

What have I walked into? Is this a homecoming, or a prelude to an assassination? He would know soon enough.

A prince. Liall was a prince.

Scarlet was quiet in the corridor after they were given leave to withdraw, a silence made up of sheer amazement, shock, and a growing sense of anger. Liall was equally silent, but his reasons were unknown to Scarlet.

A prince. Liall was a prince! I'm a pedlar, a petty merchant who sells pins and silk ribbons and perfume and cheap jewelry from town to town, and he... we...

It made Scarlet feel faintly sick.

Liall curtly gestured that Scarlet should follow him, and he started off confidently into the depths of the palace, the crowds of jeweled onlookers parting for them like the sea. Scarlet followed, staying close to Liall's side.

"These are my apartments," Liall said some endless time later, when they had walked what would have amounted to a long evening's stroll in Lysia. "Or they were, when I was a boy."

Scarlet had followed him in a daze, past gilded doorways and glittering stairs, and finally they had arrived at an enclave that could have safely held four or even five houses of the size he had grown up in, and Liall called it 'apartments'.

In merchant caravans, Scarlet had seen rare and costly things, but just the little ante-chamber of Liall's apartment put those wares to shame: richly patterned carpets and woven tapestries, crystal vases and beaded curtains, and inside there was more. There was a sitting area, like a common room back home, furnished with a green couch with deep cushions and several large chairs, each big enough for a grown man to curl up in like a baby. Tall chests paneled in dark-tinted wood lined the walls, and there was some type of game table surrounded by a set of chairs. Small, potted vases of red flowers, in appearance almost like roses, were placed about the room, but their scent was decidedly unfamiliar. Scarlet peered to the right as they walked in and saw a wide table and delicate, carved chairs set up in an alcove lit with candles, a private dining nook of some sort, but filled with furniture far costlier than any he had seen before.

Liall signaled Scarlet to follow as he entered through an open archway into a bedroom that seemed to be made simply to house the enormous curtained bed within. The outer layers of the bedcurtains were velvet, and the inner veils were of a light-spun material like gauze or spider webs. The sheets on the bed looked like silk and were dyed crimson with crushed carilla shells. The deep, red color with its characteristic shadings of black and purple was unmistakable, and there was much of it scattered around these rooms. Carilla was the most expensive of dyes, imported from far across the sea, and Scarlet used to wonder where it came from. Now he knew.

However dark it was outside, it was bright within these rooms, with the light of many lamps chasing back the shadows and a fire roiling in the hearth. The blue crystal lamps looked like gigantic sapphires hollowed out to hold oil, and there were heavy woolen draperies that extended from ceiling to floor. A very large, curved casement with a glass window was behind the bed, its heavy draperies flung open to reveal a dim landscape of ice and drifting snow. The sheer size of it made him feel slightly sick. There were only two glass windows in all of Lysia. Or there had been.

A very old man, blue-eyed with a shock of wiry silver hair, and with the kindest face Scarlet had seen yet, came into the bedroom and greeted Liall. Liall took both the old man's hands before embracing him for several long moments, Scarlet saw the glisten of tears in the old man's eyes and wondered who he was. They exchanged more words and the old man lifted his chin.

"This is Nenos," Liall said, introducing the elderly one, who bowed to Scarlet. Scarlet bowed back awkwardly, and Nenos nodded politely before turning and exiting through a narrow doorway near the wall. The apartments were like a maze, and Scarlet wondered if he would get lost in them.

Liall tossed his beautiful cloak over a chair and sat down on a bench near the foot of the bed to remove his boots. "I want a bath," he said wearily. "And so do you."

He did, as a matter of fact, so he knelt to remove his own boots while Liall waited impatiently. "Why didn't you tell me?" Scarlet asked lowly.

"What reason was there until now?" Liall's tone was sharp.

Scarlet kept his head down and finished with the boots. Liall rose and signaled imperiously for Scarlet to follow. They walked barefoot through the smaller doorway into the next room, which seemed to be an undersized version of the common room, but more cozy and intimate, with a small hearth and a wide window at the back. This room was lined with shelves and shelves of books, and there was a deep, comfortable couch and several chairs.

Scarlet slowed and would have lingered in this restful room, but Liall threw an annoyed look over his shoulder. Scarlet hurried to catch up to him: through another doorway into a narrow room tiled in herringbone brick with thick rugs scattered about. There were chests and shelves, but nowhere to sit, and Liall went straight through the doorway at the back with Scarlet following, where the pedlar stopped dead in fresh shock. This brightly-lit room was large and warm and held an enormous sunken tub big enough for ten, already full of steaming water, a tall stack of towels the color of snow, and four servants, including the old man Liall had embraced.

Scarlet hesitated before entering further, but Liall allowed the servants to take his coat off and begin unbuttoning his shirt. He signaled for Scarlet to do the same, but Scarlet balked and stepped back when the servants reached out to him.

The servants were confused and turned questioning gazes on Liall for guidance. Liall gave Scarlet a warning look and shook his head slightly.

"Do as I do," Liall said in a commanding tone, and began to undress.

Scarlet nervously began to remove clothing that was stiff with salt in places. They both stank of the journey, and it would be good to be cleaner than a wash with a bucket of cold water would allow, but all these servants! Bathhouses were common in Morturii, but there a man undressed himself, unless the reputation of the house was not to be repeated in polite company. There was a name for body-servants in a bathhouse, and it was not a nice one.

Scarlet waited until Liall had climbed into the bath before he peeled off his breeches to climb in, certain his skin was flaming red before he even touched the hot water. He sank up to his chin in the bath.

A very young man with a round face like a moon, naked to the waist, knelt on the floor behind Scarlet and touched his hair. The boy wore his own pale hair tied back with ribbon. Scarlet flinched, jerking away.

"He wants to wash your hair," Liall said.

Scarlet began to say that he could damn well wash his own hair, but when he saw the set of Liall's jaw and reckoned how much it might have affected Liall to see his kin again, Scarlet submitted.

At least, he thought, I don't have to allow anyone to bathe me. When the boy came close with a bath cloth, Scarlet scowled at him until he retreated. Scarlet held out his hand for the cloth. The servants all saw the four fingers on his left hand, and that provoked a few shocked comments, but Liall would not translate.

"It is superstition," he said dismissing it.

Then Scarlet had to be quiet and tip his head back for the moon-faced boy – he heard Liall call him Chos – to work. Chos said something in his own tongue, his tone awestruck, and several of them answered.

Liall almost smiled, and this time he told Scarlet what was said: "They marvel at your fair skin and black hair. Here, we have tales of the long ago when this kingdom's dominion reached far to the south. Our warriors would raid a western land called Hiberna and steal away the most beautiful maidens and the most handsome of youths." He dunked his head under the water momentarily to wet it for washing.

"Oh, those," Scarlet said, squeezing his eyes shut to keep the soap out. "We have tales like that, but they're of the Shining Folk who came to steal away daughters and sons so that they might have children of their own."

"Just so," Liall agreed.

Scarlet opened his eyes and stared at Liall. "Your people are the Shining Folk?"

"Not now." Liall nudged Scarlet's thigh with his foot. "But then."

That made no sense at all, and Scarlet subsided into confusion. Liall stroked Scarlet's thigh again with his foot, and Scarlet pushed him away, highly embarrassed and aware that everyone had seen the caress. Liall did not seem to care.

Chos rinsed his hair carefully and squeezed the water out between two of the towels, twisting gently inside the cloth, and then spoke to Liall. Scarlet already hated that he knew none of the native tongue here and had failed so completely at Liall's attempts to teach it to him. He resolved to take up the lessons again, in earnest this time.

Liall nodded and answered. Chos bowed and withdrew for a moment. Scarlet craned his head around to see Chos return with a comb made of fine tortoiseshell.

"Liall," he complained.

"Let him attend you," Liall said, and his tone was again short. "You are not in Byzantur now."

Chos was careful with the snags, and it was actually rather restful, except that, while Chos was still untangling him, Liall rose from the bath.

"Where are you going?"

Liall dried his face on a towel, looking like a tower of carved, water-dewed amber in the lamplight, and Scarlet was embarrassed that Liall seemed unconcerned at being naked with so many people in the room. The servants could have been invisible, or even a mirror by the way he was showing his body off to them! Scarlet suffered a pang of jealousy as Liall slipped into the robe that another handsome servant held for him.

"I must speak to my mother before I sleep tonight. Nenos will see to your needs. Try to get some rest."

Scarlet began to rise, but the comb snagged him tight. "Ow! You're leaving?"

Liall gave him an impatient look. "For a little while. There are answers I must have, and I cannot get them sitting in a tub. Finish your bath. You will be quite safe here."

"When are you coming back?"

Liall looked angry for a moment. "In due time."

Scarlet swallowed his protests and sank back into the hot water. Safe, he thought. Always 'safe'. It's a wonder how many times I've nearly been killed after someone said that.

Liall went into the outer room, which Scarlet learned later was a dressing room. Nenos followed. Scarlet heard them speaking, but could not understand a word of it. He could not understand a word from any of them, and sudden unease made his heart thud a little faster. Everyone at home knew enough Bled or Morturii or even Minh to make themselves understood, but this language was unlike anything he had ever heard. Liall had told Scarlet already how his people guarded their solitude, venturing out only for certain trade items and allowing no foreigners in. The few lands that saw trade from here had to rely on native traders to bring out what they craved.

Scarlet had always enjoyed strange surroundings and did not mind being the only foreigner here, but he hated not being able to understand what people were saying. Liall's abrupt departure felt like being abandoned, never mind that he was only going to see his mother who was a Queen. *A Queen!* Scarlet felt a fresh rush of mortification. He had no more business in front of a Queen than a mouse in front of an eagle.

The servants seemed to sense his distress. They went silent until Chos had finished with his hair. The boy signed that he should get out, and Scarlet took the towels out of Chos's hands rather than allowing the servant to dry him. They fetched him a nightshirt made of something that felt silky on his skin, but was the color of old linen. Chos also brought a warmed robe that bore silk edging on the throat and breast. It dripped with embroidery and gilt thread, and the sleeves were far too long. Scarlet remembered with a pang of longing how little Annaya had tried so hard to get the stitches that Linhona taught her right. They both would have goggled like daft sheep at the garment he now wore. He touched it with a fingertip, sliding his hand over the rough surface of brilliant, knotted threads. It did not even look real. Nothing here did.

Scarlet would have liked to dress again, but they had taken his clothes and he could not make them understand enough to bring them back. The old man led him back into the bedroom and insisted on summoning a lanky man with thinning white hair and extremely long hands to inspect the cut on Scarlet's face.

"It's healing, no worry," Scarlet said, wincing as the man – Scarlet supposed he was some kind of curae – pinched and pressed his skin. "There's nothing to be done now."

The curae seemed to agree with him and shrugged. He left after some words with Nenos, and the old man bowed him out and then returned. Nenos signed to Scarlet that he should go to sleep, but he was too unsettled and the bed was enormous, with silk sheets and furs piled over the velvet. He thought he might sink if he tried to lie down.

Nenos bowed and departed. Scarlet peeked through the archway and saw that they all seemed to have gone, melted away from the apartments through some hidden doorway and swallowed up by the enormous palace around them.

He found a chair and sat in it with his hands folded. This is a fine thing, he thought irritably. Stuck in here like a baby put to bed, and not even a cup of chel He had no idea where his traveling pack had gone, and all of his things. They could be anywhere.

In a few minutes, Scarlet's natural curiosity won out over his irritation, and he began to investigate the apartment, poking in corners and looking into the closet, which was paneled in cedar and also enormous, but there seemed to be only one place made for a body to sleep in the whole place. He went back through the cozy little room and stood looking at the elegant bed, the thick pillows and covers and furs, the double layers of draperies hung over the canopy, and he felt slightly sick again.

No one here was mistaken about his place with Liall. They all knew, and for the first time it occurred to him that, in this place, he could not escape being seen as a lover of men.

Liall takes no pains at all to hide it, he thought, and he... will he be angry at me if I do? What does it mean in Rshan if one man loves another, how is it looked upon? Is it thought normal here? What if it isn't? What will Liall do then, and do I even get a say?

The blazing fire made the room too warm after the cold of the sea, and it was too splendid, too overwhelming. Scarlet could not bring himself to sit down, but paced the room back and forth, his arms crossed over his chest.

Nenos, the old servant, returned soundlessly and stood in the doorway. He watched Scarlet worriedly for a moment before vanishing into an outer room. A short time later, a different servant brought a tray of food that held small, boiled eggs and thick slices of bread, and though Scarlet was hungry as a wolf and sick to death of rancid fish and journeycake, he could only pick at it under their very watchful eyes. He found himself wondering how great folk could abide people with them every moment, staring, watching, nothing unobserved. The plates were odd little things, square rather than round, with scalloped cuts around the edges like little moons. They were painted in great detail, almost as much as the tapestries on the walls, and he found himself being careful with the fork, lest he scratch one of the designs. He had thought Hilurins loved color and detail, but these Rshani made his people's art look childish and plain in comparison. He recognized several motifs from the tapestries that he had seen before in Byzan paintings, and their construct was very similar. Perhaps it was true, what Liall said, for their art did seem to copy Rshani methods, and maybe his people really had lived here once. It gave him a strange feeling just thinking about it.

Perhaps the servants thought the first dish was not pleasing, for another appeared. The food was foreign, but good: little dumplings, both cold and hot, with some spiced meat mixture inside. The cold ones were fruit or some kind of vegetable Scarlet did not recognize. There were small bowls of sauce for dipping them, a pitcher of what tasted like spring water sweetened with berry juice, and a bottle of wine. Scarlet decided to keep a clear head and left the wine, drinking only the rosy-sweet water. He tasted one of the cold dumplings, for curiosity's sake, but when he did, his appetite returned with a vengeance and he left the plates empty.

The old man nodded in approval and had the tray taken away when Scarlet signed that he was finished.

"Thank you," Scarlet said. The servant seemed to understand the intent if not the words. Nenos smiled again and shepherded everyone out, leaving Scarlet in peace at last. By that time, he was sleepy from the bath and the food, and yet the bed seemed to loom ominously. He could not bring himself to do more than stroke a hand over the furs and silks, and their softness seemed to taunt him.

Ever since I was a boy, Scarlet thought, I've known my secret heart and known what I wanted in love, but I've always been afraid of seeking it out, because it meant that I'd be less than myself. In Byzantur, people would've pitied me or been disgusted or they would have laughed. So, I denied everything and drowned my desire in wandering. Now that I've finally given in to my heart, my worst fears – among them being seen like a petted whore strung with beads – are coming true, and these clothes and that bed make me look the part. Great Deva, how did I come to be here?

Scarlet was a pedlar from Byzantur, not some lord or prince. What would Liall's people think, seeing him at their prince's side? Hells, what would *Liall* think, suddenly back among the richness that was his birthright: glittering lords, tall and handsome, and tall, beautiful ladies, and Scarlet in his leather jacket and hood, with his scarred face?

The embroidered folds at the hem of his robe were long, and if he did not take care, they would trip him up. It must have belonged to Liall at one time. Everything in this room was Liall's, including Scarlet, from the overly-attentive way the servants behaved. Was that how they saw him, as a pampered pet? Something they must keep clean and warm and fed because it belonged to their master? It was the crew of the Ostre Sul all over again, just in better lodgings.

Scarlet brooded as the night wore on and Liall did not reappear, and he was tired. Finally, he curled up on the thick, clean wool of the hearth rug, pillowed his head on his arm and sank into sleep.

"They told me you'd come back, brother."

The voice belonged to the man Liall believed responsible for both the bravos at Volkovoi and the pirate attack at sea. The barons were already in the palace, having arrived weeks ago to Nadiushka's summons. It was well, for there was no time to waste. Already, many had openly declared for Cestimir, but an equal amount had voiced either doubt or a marked preference for Vladei, the other contender for the crown.

Strictly speaking, Vladei and he were cousins. Vladei was the son of Liall's father's half-brother, and ostensibly Liall's step-brother now as well, since Nadiushka had solved a particularly thorny situation regarding the succession by marrying Vladei's father soon after Liall had left Rshan.

The man had not changed. Vladei, Baron of Uzna Minor. His father had been a prince. By inclusion, Vladei was now also a prince, but he did not carry the Queen's name. He and Liall had never been friends, and when Liall was twenty and suddenly engaged to the Lady Shikhoza, what little cordiality there was between them quickly vanished. Vladei had always loved her.

Vladei was standing with his younger brother, Eleferi, near the entrance to the Queen's chambers. Vladei stared at Liall as if he were some beast crawling on his good furniture, and Eleferi's fox-like face was frozen into an affable mask that had never fooled anyone. Liall was not gladdened to see his step-brothers. Absence does not always make the heart grow fonder.

Vladei was entitled to wear silver and blue, the royal colors, being ap kyning, a child born of kings, but he had eschewed them for the red and gold of Ramung's house, Vladei's grandfather as well as Eleferi's. Liall wondered idly if Vladei remembered that Ramung was only half royal, the child of a slave concubine and a king, and if he were making some point by refusing to wear the Queen's colors. Was Vladei tipping his hand already, letting it be known that his vote – and his soldiers – would be thrown against Nadiushka when the time came? Surely not. Vladei was smarter than that.

The deep, golden silk of the long hapcoat – a sort of sleeveless winged over-mantle slit up the back and sides – that Vladei wore over his crimson virca complimented his coloring. There was red piping on Vladei's sleeve and a circle of grain sheaves embroidered in darker gold, the symbol of his grandmother's country; Hessiau, Baroness of S'geth. Clearly, Vladei wished no one to forget that he was as royal as any man at court.

Vladei looked less sour than Liall remembered, and for the first time Liall realized that the many people who used to say that the two of them looked very much alike were correct. Blood will out, they say, and Vladei looked enough like Liall that he could see where people would comment. Both his step-brothers had snow-pale hair, the coveted color of the Lukaska line, but Eleferi was merely a smaller, silkier version of his brother, with sharp, sly features and a reputation for over-indulgence in sex and wine.

Vladei's features were much closer to Liall's. Only their eyes were different. Liall's were pale blue; Vladei's were chips of cloudy stone. His nose was a bit bigger than Liall's, and he had a distracting habit of twisting his rings around and around his bony knuckles when he spoke. There were also rumors that he had poisoned his latest mistress and was viciously opposed to allowing the very young Lady Ressilka to come to court. Fearing, many thought, her father, Ressanda was the Baron of Tebet and unswervingly loyal to the Queen, and thus to Cestimir. One heard his strong-willed daughter was of the same mind.

Liall nodded at him. "Vladei."

Vladei stared at Liall's simple clothing pointedly. Liall had chosen to wear only a plain blue virca – a sort of skirted tunic with long sleeves – with black breeches and shirt, and no badge of office or royal insignia.

"Nazheradei." Vladei toyed with a string at his sleeve and did not exactly meet Liall's gaze, and his voice was exactly as Liall remembered. "So it is true: you are here. At this time, I would normally make the appropriate comment about prodigal sons and joyous homecomings, but you don't look very joyous."

"And almost not very prodigal," Liall returned. "There were unfortunate incidents that nearly delayed my arrival. You knew long ago, did you not, that the Queen would send for me? Or, should I say, you feared it?"

"You wrong my brother, Nazheradei," Eleferi interjected, and then closed his pointed jaw with a snap when Vladei whipped his head round to glare at him. The years had been less than kind to Eleferi, who was a bit plump, although he was still sleekly handsome. Rather like an overfed seal.

"Wronged him, how?" Liall looked from one closed expression to the other. "Odd. You seem to know already what incidents I'm referring to."

"My brother is overly zealous on my behalf," Vladei slid in smoothly. "Pay no mind. But tell me, have you been made comfortable?" He asked this like an innkeeper asks a guest he would rather be rid of, and quickly. "Rshan is not like Byzantur at all, I'm afraid. Not what you're accustomed to."

Liall gritted his teeth. "I am quite well cared for, thank you. My needs are few. I came because my mother summoned me. Nothing else could have induced me to return."

"Ah, then I take it you will be leaving us soon? After you have seen to your mother's business?"

"I will leave when I'm satisfied that all she wishes of me has been fulfilled. Not before."

"And if it proves impossible to accommodate the Queen?" Eleferi interjected.

Liall slid Eleferi a look that shut him up. "In case you haven't learned this yet, heed me: One does not say *no* to a queen."

Vladei continued to twist his rings. One, a thick gold

band bearing a sapphire the size of a robin's egg, Liall recognized as once belonging Vladei's father, Lankomir. Vladei stared at Liall's hands in return, and saw that he wore no jewelry save the ring of State sent to him via the Minh courier. Vladei's shifting eyes lit on the leather necklace of two copper coins partially hidden beneath Liall's black collar.

"A strange token for a prince to wear," Vladei commented.

Liall felt an urge to cover the coins with his hand, as if Vladei could dirty them somehow. He kept still. "It holds a meaning for me."

"Two worthless coins?" Vladei asked, suddenly sharp. "And you brought a Hilurin here to pollute our halls. Are you insane, to put the royal family in such danger?"

Liall almost allowed his temper to flare, and he forced himself to take a steadying breath. "You must not have heard, Vladei, and who can blame you? You have been occupied with affairs of state, and I commend you on your diligence. Let me inform you then: the Hilurin is my t'aishka." Liall fought to keep his voice low and even. "He is my t'aishka and his name is mine. His honor is mine. Of course, you did not know this, so we must let this unintended insult pass."

Deprived of this tack, Vladei took another. "They are our enemies. They stole the power of the Shining Ones and made them mortal."

"Nonsense!" Liall scoffed. "That moldy old legend. You can't possibly believe it."

"Melev believes it," Vladei said, naming one of the Ancients of Fanorl Nauhin, a healer and a man respected almost as much as the queen. "They brought our race down. Did Alexyin teach you in vain?"

"We brought our race down," Liall corrected. "It was pride and cruelty that wasted the powers of the Shining

Ones. As for myself, I am neither immortal nor magical, and so I do not care. It was very long ago and it has nothing to do with me."

Out of the corner of his eye, Liall spied Lady Shikhoza coming down the great lamp-lit hallway. Vladei, too watched her with his flat eyes. He had been in love with Shikhoza since she was a girl. She, for her part, had not loved him in the least, but Vladei had not known that. Neither had she loved Liall, but he had not known either. They had much more in common than pedigree, Vladei and him, though it did not endear them to one another.

One does not quarrel in front of court women, and Liall turned just as Shikhoza approached. He gave her a small bow, folding his arm over his waist in the Rshani fashion. Shikhoza, lady of Jadizek and Nau Karmun, with a lineage as venerable as the Queen she had once sought to be. Her beauty – like ice, but with none of its ability to change – was dimmed but still evident. Her hair was the palest gold, piled high on her head and held with pins of diamond and chalcedony. Below them her eyes, the lids painted with blue cosmetics like most women at court, were sharp chips of oyster gray, and her face was as carved and perfect as a statue. Far from vanishing, her looks had frozen around her, calcified by bitterness and disappointment into a mask of lifeless beauty.

Liall searched his feelings as he looked long at her, relieved that he felt nothing at all. He was not even angry with her.

Like all Rshani women, Shikhoza wore a *tarica:* a voluminous, long-sleeved dress that tied and laced quite tightly to a woman's shape to just under her breasts, and then fell in endless pleats and wide folds to her ankles. Walking, Rshani court women seemed to glide inside these capacious garments, endlessly graceful and stately. In her hand she held a small bit of silken embroidery stretched around a silver frame, a golden needle pinned through it.

"You called him t'aishka," Shikhoza said, voice sliding out of her as smoothly as mist.

Liall had forgotten her voice, how wondrously fair it was, and was nettled that it had not aged the way her looks had.

"That is rare for a Byzan, even a Byzan concubine."

Liall bowed his head, showing respect for her station if not for her person. "Shikhoza."

She bent her head. "Nazheradei."

"He's not a concubine," Liall continued smoothly. He wondered how many times he was going to have this conversation regarding Scarlet.

"Your slave, then. Or your servant."

"Neither. We met as adversaries and became friends. He is my t'asihka, my forever beloved, as you well heard."

"Heard but can scarce believe." She laughed, a high, tinkling mirth, showing him the polished whiteness of her teeth. She declined to greet either Vladei or Eleferi, and Liall wondered at that. "What, are there no women across the sea?"

"There are indeed."

She had nothing to say to that. Perhaps she fears what my answer will be, Liall thought. "You still have your place at court," he said, hiding his surprise.

"I do."

"I cannot imagine that the Queen has forgiven you."

"Oh, she has not," Shikhoza said with emphasis. "She despises me as deeply as she ever did. But she needs me."

"She needs your title, Lady."

Shikhoza shrugged her shoulders within the voluminous satin. "They are one and the same. We hate each other, but between her crown and my lands, a king might be made."

Liall was all too aware that Vladei and Eleferi were listening. "And the name of that king?"

Shikhoza looked down at her handiwork – a small rendering of a swan – and her painted mouth curved in a small smile. "I remember when you called me t'aishka."

"I never called you that."

"No? Perhaps I imagined it, then. Young girls consider the t'aishka legend quite romantic, and I was very young, and much given to listening to superstition and foolishness."

The intended slight to his devotion to Scarlet did not anger Liall, but neither did he pity her. All Shikhoza had hoped for in life had come down to this: the maiden spinster, lady-in-waiting to an old Queen, a fractious and degenerate court, and nothing to do all day but spin plots and lies. He did not pity her, for spinning lies was what she was good at, but he did finally look at her, and she at him.

Sixty-three years it had been. He had never lost count. They had aged, the both of them, though Liall thought he looked the worse for wear. She was no girl anymore, no tender blossom ripe for plucking, but she was still beautiful. It made him sad, for there was no beauty in her eyes, no kindness, and not the least bit of softness. He had faced enemies in battle who met his eyes with less hatred.

Liall girded himself and offered her his arm to escort her to her station, which formerly had been inside the Queen's second tier chamber; the customary place for a lady of her high rank. Eleferi bowed properly, but Vladei only stepped aside in silence, trying to catch her eye, to get her to notice him. She lifted her chin, slid her arm smoothly in Liall's and glided past Vladei without a glance. Liall caught a glimpse of Vladei's expression as they passed, expecting to see him spitting mad, but Vladei gazed on Shikhoza with an expression of sorrow. Liall nearly stumbled in surprise. After all these years, to realize that his step-brother had a heart would take some getting used to.

Then they were away from his step-brothers and strolling toward the next set of doors, her hand clasping his forearm, and his hand placed over hers. It was formality only, but with his nerves so raw, it felt far more intimate.

"How was your journey?" she inquired. Her manner seemed changed when they were away from Vladei, and Liall recalled that she had always loathed the man.

"Four months of cold water, rats, and bad food."

"And you wanted me to go with you at one time. How do you think I would have fared out there, the mariner of a rough ship on the frozen sea?"

Liall thought it over. "You would have cut your hair and donned breeches, and been managing the crew with an iron hand within a week."

She laughed for real and her hand tightened on his arm. "Think you so? Well, I might have indeed. We will never know now. Still," she gave him a fetching look "it would have been an adventure."

This woman had been at least partly to blame for Liall's exile, and it galled him to hear her painting the matter so differently from fact. He pulled away from her a little. "My departure from Rshan was no adventure, lady."

Her expression fell and that glass brow wrinkled. "No," she intoned. "And lest you think me heartless, Nazheradei... I do remember."

Spite he could deal with, but Liall did not know this repentant woman, and it bested him. "You did imagine many things, long ago, but I did once say that I loved you," Liall confessed tiredly. "Yet that was before you poured poison into my brother's ear against me. You wanted me to cast him down so you would be called Queen. Well, I did, but not in the way you planned. This is what your plotting has brought you to. Are you content?"

She looked again to her embroidery and traced the swan with the round, painted tip of her thumbnail. "I wonder," she said slowly, as if the matter caused her much worry. "I wonder how much of your love for this Hilurin has to do with who he is, and how much of it has to do with how different he is from me."

The Queen's door opened and Liall could see Bhakamir, the Queen's aide, motioning him to come inside. Liall looked at Shikhoza and reminded himself that he had once intended to take this Lady as his wife. It made his words much less harsh than they would have been. Liall pushed her off his arm and returned her hand, not roughly, but with a firmness that said she would never have that place again.

"My lady," he said. "You are correct on one count at least; he is nothing at all like you."

The King had called her sunya, his star, so the stories say, and Liall did not doubt them. Though her body had finally succumbed to the ravages of age and infirmity, no one could doubt that Nadiushka, daughter of Lukaska, had once been a magnificent woman. She was still a magnificent Queen, but that was altogether different from being a woman.

Lindolanen and Nadiushka had married very young, two princes drunk with love and joy, and it had lasted all of three blissful years before he was killed on a snow bear hunt, torn in half by the beast's claws before his pain-mad horse dragged his blood over the snow. Nadei was too young to remember and Liall had still been in Nadiushka's belly. The Queen almost had the snow bear stricken from the Rshan coat of arms that day, but forestalled. She did do it, years later, after another tragedy involving the same type of beast struck the royal court again. The snow bear had ever been unlucky for his family. A curse, some say, though Liall did not believe in such things any more than he believed in magic.

Nadiushka was seated on a lesser throne made of dark wood and silver, set on a polished wooden dais with three steps that served as her informal audience chair. She tapped her slippered foot, indicating that Liall should sit upon the wide platform of the throne, up the steps and near her feet. Liall obeyed, and she regarded him searchingly.

"The man I married after your father died has died himself," his mother said.

Liall had known this from the time he left Volkovoi. "I never much liked Lankomir," Liall said casually, knowing that his mother shared the sentiment. Lankomir, Lindolanen's half-brother, was father to Vladei and Eleferi. Their mother had been a southern princess, now dead, and Lankomir had been an unpleasant, dull-witted man, greedy and prideful. Lankomir had, however, given Nadiushka a child: Cestimir, the boy whom she planned to make king.

"He is dead," she repeated, seeming pleased to say it. "This you know. Now, what you do not know: you do not know that Cestimir is fit to be king. I have kept him close to me since his birth, and I have watched him, and he is worthy."

Liall bowed his head shortly, accepting his mother's words. To his knowledge, she had never been wrong about anything. He was not going to start doubting her now.

"At fourteen, he is yet still too young to rule, and too

inexperienced," she said. "The latter will pass quickly once he begins to take charge of the realm. What you do not know is that there have been several attempts on Cestimir's life since my... my second husband died. There can be only one cause for this."

"Someone does not want him to inherit the throne."

"And you do not have to look far to guess who that someone might be. They are all within these very walls." Her brittle smile was small and endlessly bitter.

"Are there any you suspect more than others, my mother?"

She looked at her hands. "Must I say it?"

"You must."

Her eyes glittered. "I have known them since they were boys. How could they?"

Liall had no answer for her, but he still needed to hear it out loud. He must be sure. "Vladei and Eleferi?"

Her stepsons, Cestimir's own half-brothers. She nodded wordlessly, taking deep, steadying breaths with her hand fluttering near her heart. Bhakamir was instantly at her side, silently offering her a clear vial that contained some pale liquid or medicine. She waved him away.

"But... you are *ill*," Liall said, suddenly alarmed. He had never in his life seen his mother sick. "Why have you not sent for Melev?"

"He has been," she sighed. "There is nothing he can do. Even *he* cannot stave off death forever."

By practice, Melev was an Rshani healer, but he was more than that. He was the culmination of a genesis that began the Rshani race as Liall knew it. Melev was not a Shining One, but neither was he quite mortal.

"He should be by your side—" Liall began, but her chin came up and the old, fierce light was in her eyes.

"I need no crutch!"

Indeed she did not. Queen for over a hundred years,

and more than half that time she had been forced to reign alone or with a powerless consort at her side.

She counted on her sons to relieve her of the burden, Liall thought, but we both failed her, I most of all.

Liall struggled to speak. It had been so long, so many years ago, yet in front of his mother it seemed like yesterday...

Nadei's sword broken on the tiles, kneeling with his hand pressed to his side, and that white look of shock on his face as the red blood poured out from under his palm and down his leg, a bright lake forming about his knees while their mother screamed and screamed...

"Forgive me, Mother," Liall whispered starkly. He could not look at her. She was silent for a moment, and then he felt her warm hand on the crown of his head.

"Nazheradei, I forgave you the day I banished you."

Liall held back from weeping like the child he suddenly felt to be, but only just. They both retreated to their corners of silence and she withdrew her hand. He ached for that touch, but he had no rights anymore, no claim on her love.

She sighed. "You must have guessed why I sent for you."

Liall nodded. It had been obvious. That did not mean he had to like it. "I don't know how much use I can be. There will be few nobleman who will side with Cestimir, and with me, none."

"You are wrong to think that, but no matter. It's not a question of persuading them to side with me or with you or even with the side of justice or the good of Rshan. No, we have only to convince them that their own interests will not be served by supporting Vladei, and that Cestimir is the more profitable choice. Once they are made to see that, we will have them." She clenched her bony fingers into a fist.

"The way to a baron's heart is through his wallet," Liall quoted wryly. "I remember your lessons, Mother." He shrugged. "But the barons also remember. They remember me. They remember Nadei. I may do your cause more harm than good."

She shrugged and clasped her hands in her lap. "And yet, you are my only hope. We must both do what we can. It is my duty to Cestimir and your duty to me. Will you shirk that?"

Liall shook his head. "You know I will not. I am yours to command."

She finally gave him a real smile, the first one he had seen from her since his boyhood, years before he left Rshan. "My son, I knew that before I sent for you."

Liall could not answer.

She regarded him with her too-wise eyes, noting every new scar, every line in his face that was not there when he left.

"You have prospered among the lenilyn?" She shook her head, not waiting for him to answer. "Of all the lands of Nemerl, child, why the Southern Continent? Why not the jeweled empire of Hiberna, the exotic island kingdoms of the Serpent Sea? Why that desolate and accursed place?"

"Exile is intended as punishment. I would not have it said that I used my prince's title to escape my doom and seek comfort from the kings of the west."

Her chest moved up and down with a steadying breath. "We only learned you were alive and in Byzantur five years ago. I have suffered much, knowing you spent so many years in that place. Tell me... how did you make a life there?"

"By becoming one of them," Liall said simply. "The people there are as varied as anywhere on Nemerl. They have honor and good in them, but also greed and savagery and pettiness of heart." Liall ducked his head. "I fear I found my place with them in the seedier circles of the Kasiri bandits, but it was not a bad life, all in all. There were many people I was fond of. Also, the little Hilurins are not the sly demons our legends make them out to be." He looked up at her guardedly. "It was a life," he repeated. "A simpler one than I had growing up. All my enemies come at me with knives instead of smiles, and they are not half so clever to hide what they feel."

"So life is easier for you out there."

"I wouldn't go that far."

She smirked in amusement, but her eyes were barbed. It had always been this way between them, this easy and bantering manner that hid so many thorns and hurts. Liall had not missed this part of their relationship at all.

"And yet," she went on "there are comforts."

Liall knew what she meant, or rather, whom. He nodded.

"How is he called again?"

"Scarlet," Liall supplied, repeating it for her twice. She tried it out, pursing her lips over the feel of it.

"What does it mean, precisely? It is not a Bizye word."

"Not from the known tongue, no. I believe it is part of the northern dialect from the river towns. It means simply red, albeit a very pretty shade, the color of carmine or a deep red rose."

"Or of blood."

"Do not say such things," Liall begged, remembering his dream of the bear hunt and Scarlet's body covered in blood.

"Alas, morbidity has become my habit." She was silent for a moment, then; "Why do they call him that? He is not red."

"I think it is a poetic appellation, something to do with a spirited nature."

"Ah," she said archly. "Now we have it. And do you find him spirited?"

Liall remembered Scarlet in the Volkovoi alleyway, facing down two armed bravos who were twice his size. "Yes."

"Raja," she said. Crimson. "That would be his name in Sinha, yes?"

"Somewhat. But do you know the little flame flower that grows by the sea? And the red color of its petals, and when we say a person is fiery, they are *keriss*? That is closer to it, I think." Liall did not think her questioning odd. Names were very important in Rshan.

She slapped her hands together very softly, glad to have it settled. "That is his court name, then: Keriss *kir* Nazheradei." She tilted her head. "How did he come to be so recently scarred?"

"On the journey that brought us here," Liall said shortly.

"Ah," she said archly. "This would have happened aboard the ship, then."

Liall sighed. "Yes, madam, but since you already know how it happened, I fail to comprehend why you trouble yourself to question me about the matter."

"Perhaps because I wonder that you would expose someone you profess to care about to such danger. Was the experience with the mariners not enough proof for you? And yet, still you brought this Hilurin child to our shores, knowing what could happen. Why?"

"What else was I to do?" Liall snapped. "Throw him overboard? The journey was already well underway, and he is, as you said, young and inexperienced. I could not just abandon him on some distant shore." He withheld the other information: the matter of Cadan's killing and Scarlet's possible death-sentence in Byzantur. "Scarlet is my t'aishka. That settles it," Liall finished.

"Keriss *kir* Nazheradei," the Queen corrected.

Liall nodded and did not argue, not even at the *kir* designation, which would be a part of Scarlet's protection here. To Liall, his lover would always be Scarlet the redcoat, the pretty, impertinent, too-proud pedlar scowling and refusing him a kiss. His spirit lightened just to think of it, and she saw this and softened.

"Your *t'aishka* is very beautiful, very charming and rare."

Liall thanked her, though it was only the truth, then he saw that she was trying to be tactful. "Say what you must, madam. You've never had difficulty before."

"He is very young, is he not? And uneducated, and a lenilyn, and a peasant. The people will not like it, Nazheradei. The nobles will not."

"Then they can choke on it."

She laughed, tossing her head like a girl. "My Nazir," she said, giving him his baby name. "So stubborn you always were. So proud and confident, never caring what others thought of you. You always went against the winds. If there was a rule, you broke it. No propriety was safe in your presence."

"Mother, I would love him if he were a prince, too," Liall pleaded. The fire crackled lowly over his protest and the blue light of the crystal lamps threw a glow on them like the moon over water. It had grown very late. "I do care what some people think, you know," Liall admitted. "I want you to like him."

"I know, but I will make up my own mind on this account. He will not sit at the High Table just yet. That is too much favor for a foreigner whom I know nothing of."

"Except that I love him."

"Your heart is your province, my lord, but I rule here."

"And you accuse me of pride, Mother?" He heard the haughty tone in her voice and knew it was pointless to argue Scarlet's virtues with her. All royalty had its blind spots. He risked putting his hand in hers. "Will the Queen inform what she requires of me?"

Nadiushka straightened her back, and Liall could see her mentally preparing herself for what lay ahead. His mother was as iron-willed as ever. He felt a flush of pride for her and knew that, no matter what happened or what it cost either of them, she was determined to see Rshan safe.

Bhakamir escorted Liall to the outer chamber. Behind him, Nadiushka slumped pale and shrunken in her chair, one hand covering her eyes. They had talked for hours, plan upon plan, allies to be trusted and those to be feared and yes, even those who would have to be eliminated if the worst happened. No milk-lily maid, her. Though Liall knew she loved him and loved Cestimir, sometimes his mother frightened him. At times, she could melt his heart with her kindness, and then she could turn around and be as ruthless as any general on a bloody battlefield.

Regent. She wanted him to be regent until Cestimir reached his majority. For an Rshani noble, that was sixteen winters. But... Regent? She wanted to step down from the throne and pass all power to him in Cestimir's name. Either she trusted him more than anyone on the face of the world or else she secretly hated Cestimir. He could not imagine how it must have been for her.

Thankfully, Shikhoza was gone from the outer chamber. At least he would not have to see that particular lady again so soon. But she had left her little embroidered swan, perhaps intentionally. Who knew? Rshani women were full of little nuances and subtleties and lies. There were layers upon layers of meaning in every conversation, complexities sewn in and around every word, hints and intricacies and far too little real meaning to any of it. Liall remembered that it used to grate on him, and bore him, and he wished for silence. Well, he had gotten that in abundance.

He smelled the little silken swan and smiled bitterly. It was her perfume, not the one she had worn tonight, but the scent he remembered from her youth, something insipidly light and smelling of flowers: a girl's perfume.

He dropped it on the bench and went to seek Scarlet and his bed, but he was stopped, again, at the outer tier. Melev was there, blocking his way.

Neither truly Rshani nor foreign, Melev towered over Liall. The Ancient was so tall that he had to duck through most doorways, and his frame was equally huge. His skin was the color of red oak, his broad, angular features seemingly carved from immutable stone, and he was bald, which was a rare thing in Rshan. He wore no boots or garments of rank, only a rough, homespun robe belted with a strip of leather around his middle. Dressed like this, Melev could walk across the frozen continent from end to end and suffer no injury or ill effects.

Melev bowed, his face frozen into solemn lines, before rising to his full height to regard Liall with frost-colored eyes as large as apricots.

"Your t'aishka," Melev said in his rolling bass voice, gesturing with one his monstrous hands, the six fingers of which moved in odd directions as he spoke. "Is it true? Is he Anlyribeth?

A proper greeting would not have occurred to Melev. Creatures like him did not think along the same polite lines as ordinary men.

"Hilurin," Liall corrected, studying him. "But yes, the same race."

Melev only nodded as if he had known it all along, his eyes glittering like moonstones. He turned abruptly and walked away with a fluid, ground-eating stride. "See you keep him well."

Liall nearly called Melev back, suddenly frightened that the Ancient had experienced some foreboding or possessed some secret knowledge, but he was away before Liall could stop him. Liall returned to his apartments with a much heavier step.

It seemed to Scarlet that he had been asleep only a moment before a light touch woke him. He started upright and there was Liall, crouched next to him. The sadness was back in Liall's eyes, and he looked older somehow.

"Scarlet, why are you sleeping on the hearth?"

Scarlet felt tongue-tied, but Liall's bizarre wardrobe loosened his speech. "What in Deva's name are you wearing?"

Liall wore a knee-length sort of skirted tunic, long-sleeved, made of rich blue wool with rows of ornamental silver buttons down both sides of his chest, rather like a dress that Annaya might wear. Scarlet was embarrassed for him, being made to dress like a girl, even though he wore breeches and boots and a black silk shirt under the contraption.

Liall laughed at his expression. "I assure you, this is what is worn in Rshan. It's called a *virca*."

Perhaps so, but Scarlet did not know this silk-clad

gentleman. This was not his Kasiri chieftain, but some stranger. Liall smiled and the strangeness fell away.

"Well, did you get your answers?"

"I haven't even begun to ask the questions," Liall sighed.

Liall ran a hand through his hair, which had grown on the voyage. It was no longer the close-cropped affair that had looked so odd to Scarlet at first. Liall's white hair reached nearly to the bottom of his ears now, and it looked much softer and altogether more comely on him.

"That woman," Scarlet began. "Your mother, is she really... are you?"

"She is a Queen, so I am by default a prince. Although," his look was heavy. "I renounced all that long ago, many years now. I am no longer Prince Nazheradei of Rshan."

"Why come back at all, then?"

"Because no matter what, I am still my mother's son. She asked me to come and I could not refuse."

"What does she want from you?"

"That," Liall said "I cannot tell you at this moment. What I can tell you is that my mother is what we call a progressive leader. She has forbidden dueling in the Nauhinir and all southern cities, loosened the trade restrictions for women, and has relaxed import regulations to allow our trade ships more freedom both to make profits and enter into trade contracts with foreigners. Her actions have caused no small amount of dissent within the realm. There are those," he said slowly, "who believe my mother has betrayed the traditions of our people, and that what she has begun, Prince Cestimir will continue. This has resulted in many fractures in the power structure of the neighboring barons in the south kingdom and has reawakened many old feuds that the great families still maintain with the north."

Scarlet could find little to say. It was all beyond him,

this talk of kingdoms and contracts. He could only nod and hold his tongue. Liall's speech sounded rehearsed and the sense of betrayal still stung him. He knew he had been lied to, but he did not know how much he could blame Liall for it. Part of him wanted to shout and accuse, and another just wanted reassurance that matters would not change between them. Though, of course, that was impossible.

Liall was no fool. "You're angry."

"Four months is a long time to sail," he answered. "In all that time, you might have given me a hint."

Liall's face was drawn with weariness. "I never asked you to come to Rshan with me, Scarlet. I knew it would be impossible. I did not tell you on the ship because there are things about me that even yet I am not ready to share with you." When Scarlet remained silent, Liall bit his lip and bowed his head. "You must admit that I could not have intentionally set out to deceive you."

Scarlet nodded. "I know. That's what makes all this so hard to believe."

Liall rose and held out his hand. He drew Scarlet up to stand with him. "We may be here for a long time," he said, holding Scarlet's hands between his. "Whatever mistakes I have made, I promise I will try to amend them. And you must trust me now, my love, no matter how angry you are with me. Your life, and probably mine, depends on it."

My love. Scarlet liked the sound of that. Suddenly, Nenos was back with lengths of pale clothing draped over his arm. The servant laid out another nightshirt and robe for Liall, and Scarlet looked at the old man with misgiving, not liking the idea of being tended waking and asleep.

Liall followed his gaze. "You must accustom yourself to Nenos. He has served me since I was a boy."

Scarlet nodded. Liall spoke to Nenos in Sinha and Scarlet heard his name. He flicked a questioning look to Liall. Nenos bowed and then left them alone, and Liall put an arm around Scarlet's shoulders and drew him toward the bed.

"I should not have allowed you to come with me," Liall said distantly, pulling him into a fierce embrace. "It is far more dangerous than even I had expected. You might have done better taking your chances with the Flower Prince's mercy."

"Too late for that now."

"Yes, of course," Liall said. He cupped Scarlet's face in both of his hands. "And I know you can take care of yourself, but while we are here, you must heed me in everything. You must guard your words; engage in no quarrels or disputes. It is far too dangerous."

"I haven't—" he began, but Liall stopped his mouth by kissing him, slow and sweet, and Scarlet could have no complaints about that.

Liall drew back and studied him gravely. "You and I, we had a bad beginning, t'aishka, and there is a part of you that still does not trust me. Yet you must, and you must heed me and be guided by me while we are here, or we both may die."

"I trust you," Scarlet said, but neither of them had forgotten how he had recoiled from Liall time and time again, how he had mistrusted the older man even in bed, and how they had once come to blows back on the Nerit. He wondered what Liall was getting at. "I do trust you," he insisted. "I just don't feel very in control here. I haven't felt in control of anything since we left Volkovoi."

Liall looked at Scarlet for a long moment. "We are going to play a game," he said seriously.

Scarlet huffed, though the corners of his mouth turned up in a smile. "What kind of game?"

"A lover's game," Liall said, and kissed him again, sliding his hand beneath the wool of the robe to caress Scarlet's skin through the silk of the nightshirt.

Scarlet shivered. "A lover's game?" He had never heard of such. "How?"

"You must not ask," Liall murmured. There was an odd look on his face as he pushed the robe from Scarlet's shoulders, letting it drop to the floor. "The only thing you must do is to command me to stop at any moment that you cease to trust me."

Scarlet was not sure he liked that, but Liall was pulling at the laces of his silken nightshirt, and he focused on removing Liall's virca, or trying to.

"It's a damned dress, it is," Scarlet muttered, and Liall laughed softly and kissed Scarlet again before drawing back to attend to the buttons of the virca himself.

Liall's hands were very warm and big. Everything about him was big: his fingers as they drew lines across Scarlet's chin and lips, his tongue that teased and tickled within Scarlet's mouth, even his sex. At no other time was Scarlet so reminded of the differences between Rshani and Hilurin as when he was intimate with Liall.

Scarlet scarcely noticed when the silken nightshirt slid to the floor and puddled at his feet, but he yelped in surprise when Liall lifted him up and tossed him on the bed to lie sprawled naked on red silks and fur.

Liall laughed. "You see, this is the point," he said, his voice low and hot as he climbed into the bed with Scarlet, leaning over him. "Did you want me to do that?"

"I have no idea."

"Well, think about it. What do you want me to do right now?"

Scarlet did not understand, yet he hardly minded. "Undress?" he asked hoarsely.

Liall leaned in for a kiss, and then sat back on his heels

and took off his black silk shirt. "Yes, my lord." His pale eyes glinted with mischief.

Scarlet watched him undress, which Liall did slowly and deliberately, holding Scarlet's gaze at all times. When he was nude, Liall took up his black shirt again and turned it this way and that, and then ripped the long collar off.

"What did you do that for?"

"Shh, trust me for a moment," Liall said, and straddled Scarlet's body with his knees. "All you have to do is order me to stop."

Scarlet nearly pulled away when Liall put the silken scrap over his eyes, on the verge of panic. He did trust Liall, or at least, he did in this. If he hesitated when they were alone, it was not lack of trust, but the fact that Liall himself could be almost overwhelming.

I do trust him, he thought. I do.

Liall tied the silk around Scarlet's eyes before gently tucking his black hair back to suckle on the spot beneath his ear. It was amazing what sensations Liall could produce on parts of him that he had not expected to be sensitive. Without sight, it felt even more intense, and Scarlet jumped when cool fingers skimmed over his bare shoulder.

"Relax. You know I would not hurt you," Liall murmured. His voice was warm and lulling. "You know this."

Scarlet took a deep breath and nodded. "I know it." It was strange, not seeing, only feeling. He was conscious of the caress of fur, of the warmth of Liall's breath on the curve of his neck, the heat of skin against skin. He turned his head blindly, seeking Liall's mouth, and was rewarded with a luxurious kiss, Liall's tongue teasing his own.

Scarlet reached to embrace him. Liall took his hand and held it. "No. Not unless you can tell me yourself what you want. What do you want me to do?"

Scarlet opened his mouth to complain, but Liall kissed him again until the words had flown away. Liall then fitted his hands around Scarlet's waist and shifted Scarlet up higher on the pillows.

Scarlet was disoriented with the blindfold, but Liall guided him, his touch gentle, and Scarlet sank back against softness. He tried to reach for Liall again, and Liall took his wrist and kissed the inside of it, touching a wet tongue to the pulse there. Scarlet squirmed, and Liall stretched Scarlet's arm out, up over his head, and looped something soft around his wrist, binding it.

Suddenly alarmed, Scarlet tried to sit up, but Liall kissed his mouth gently before forcibly pushing his shoulders back to the cushions.

"Now, this is how it is," Liall's deep voice rumbled into his ear, passionate and thick. "You must not free yourself. If you cannot bear it, then you must tell me and *I* will free you. I will do nothing that you do not command me to do." His mouth was very close to Scarlet's ear. "You think you are not in control. You are very wrong about that. I have been bound to you since we met."

Scarlet took in one shaking breath, and then another while Liall stroked his hair, thinking it over. Finally, he nodded.

"Yes? Good. Very good. I will bind your other hand now."

Oh, Deva, why did that frighten him so?

Liall stretched out Scarlet's other arm the same way, and he felt soft fabric – velvet? – looped around his wrist. When Liall drew back, Scarlet tested the bonds briefly, tugging against them, before he forced himself to stop.

"You are so beautiful," Liall whispered, and stretched out beside him. Scarlet's arousal had flagged, but Liall kissed him long and slowly until he was arching against the other man, wanting more.

"I want your hands on me," Scarlet gasped. "I want to feel your weight over me."

Liall's lips moved to his throat. He suckled at the hollow and plied his teeth to lines of Scarlet's jaw and throat until Scarlet longed to break free and wrap his body around Liall.

Liall's tongue lapped against his collarbone, and Liall shifted to straddle him, just below his hips. Scarlet groaned and had to bite his lip to stop from speaking, for Liall's weight across his thighs was too low to give him any relief.

Liall tasted him, licking down his chest. When Liall's teeth tugged gently on a nipple, Scarlet cried out and tried to push up against him, but Liall would not permit it.

"Please..." Scarlet moaned, hating the sound of his pleading voice, but not being able to stop.

"Please what?" Liall asked reprovingly, and his weight lifted.

Scarlet bit his lip, but his skin now felt cold where Liall had been. He felt Liall rise from the bed. Straining to listen, he heard only the clink of metal on metal and tensed. Scarlet jumped when Liall drew near, unheard, and touched him.

"Ah, Love," Liall said and stroked his hair. He was standing beside the bed. "If you cannot trust me, you must command me to free you."

Scarlet thought long and hard. In the interim, Liall sighed deeply and began to fumble with the knots at Scarlet's wrist.

Scarlet made a sound of dissent, jerking his bound hands away, and Liall stilled.

He heard Liall's measured breath close to him. "What is it you wish?"

Scarlet let out a shuddering sigh. "I want you to kiss me. I want to feel your body on mine, your mouth on me."

Immediately, Liall's weight sank down on the bed beside him.

"Yes," Scarlet murmured. Liall's hand learned Scarlet's face, mapping it as if Liall were the one deprived of sight. Liall rested his cheek against Scarlet's chest, and Scarlet felt the warm touch of a tongue on his nipple.

"You taste so good," Liall murmured, licking, and then switched his mouth to the other one. "I could devour you, so sweet is your skin." His fingers pinched and rolled the neglected nipple as he sucked and lapped at Scarlet's chest, until Scarlet was writhing on the bed and straining against his bonds. Liall stopped abruptly and his hands drifted down Scarlet's torso. Scarlet shivered at the ticklish touches to his belly as Liall bowed his head to scatter light kisses around the navel. Scarlet gasped and jerked when he felt Liall's fingers curling around his hard length, and then Liall planted a kiss on the crown.

His voice was broken. "Please..."

Liall did not chide him again for begging, but lazily curled his tongue around the head of Scarlet's member and sucked lightly.

Scarlet thought he might faint. He made a strangled sound of pleasure, dizzy with sensation.

"You want this?"

"Yes."

Scarlet had seen slaves offered for sale in Morturii perform such acts, and it had seemed an ugly sight to him then. But oh, he never imagined it was a thing of such pleasure! How could he have known? Liall's tongue was fire. It was ice and flame and slick, soft, delicious suction empowered with the ability to lure every nerve in his body straight to his groin.

He could happily die like this.

Scarlet's body was drawn tight as a bowstring, his legs

parted wide as he strove to push deeper into the incredible heat of Liall's mouth, but after a short time — too short! Oh Deva, don't stop, don't ever stop that! — Liall pulled away.

Scarlet groaned in mournful protest and Liall raised up to silence the sound, his hot tongue thrusting deep. Scarlet suckled on it, and Liall drew back a little. Scarlet could feel Liall's smile in the curve of his lips as they kissed. Liall's leather necklace, with its two cheap Byzan coins, brushed against Scarlet's throat, and it reminded him so much of all they had been through together that he moaned again and nipped at Liall's lip.

"Please... more."

"Not so quickly," Liall whispered, taking another kiss. "I want to make this last."

Liall got up and Scarlet heard him extinguish a few of the blue lamps, then the warm, naked length of Liall's body covered him. Scarlet pushed up with his hips, seeking to bury himself in skin, and Liall made a rumbling noise deep in his throat that sent a curl of fire down Scarlet's spine.

Liall's hands roamed. His mouth and tongue rooted out every pleasurable spot on Scarlet's body —some he had not even imagined could be pleasurable!—and Scarlet knew no more coherent thoughts. Liall learned his lover's shape so thoroughly that Scarlet thought he might be committing it to memory.

"T'aishka, what shall I do now?"

"I don't know. I don't know how, or what...." Scarlet panted. His head thrashed from side to side.

"Do you want me to go further?"

"Please. I want you to do whatever you want. I just want you. I want you, *please*...."

Then there was the smell of incense and beeswax swirling around in his head, mixed up with the feel of

Liall's mouth and hands and body, and he floated in the center of it, burning and gasping and bound, until Liall's fingers gently untied the silk that blinded him. Liall urged Scarlet to wrap his legs around Liall's waist.

Scarlet could see Liall at last: his expression of careful urgency, and how gently Liall sought to breach that entrance. Scarlet tried not to cry out as Liall continued in his delicate and deliberate conquest, but it was too much, and eventually Scarlet was shuddering and moaning steadily. Liall would freeze at each keen and gasp, but only for a moment as he coaxed Scarlet's body to gladly submit, feeding the fire in Scarlet's bones until the younger man was panting and arching up to him, pliant and hot. Then, like a prince taking a rival country, Liall would advance again, pushing closer to his goal.

One final stride, and Scarlet's last sharp, shocked cry was muffled against Liall's amber throat as their hips met and Liall let out a tortured groan, moving sinuously inside him.

He's not a wolf, he's a snake, a serpent. Scarlet's mind babbled on as Liall's body coiled and uncoiled fluid as a leopard, piercing impossibly deep.

Liall rolled his hips and lifted Scarlet, pushing in at an angle that made sparks flare in Scarlet's brain. Scarlet shouted as his body hurled onward, oblivious to who might hear, uncaring. He felt like he was dying, or living more completely than he had imagined possible.

The lamps had burned down to a blue fireflies, and Liall, his face dripping with sweat, looked down on Scarlet with wide, wondering eyes before a violent shudder seized his frame and wracked him dry, and he called out helplessly in strange, flowing words that sank liquid into the scented air.

9.

Forgive

Scarlet was cuddled up to Liall's chest, belly to belly and naked as the moon, his hair smelling musky and sweet with Rshani soap. Gods, but I hate to get out of bed this morning, Liall thought.

He wanted to wake the young man with touch, to ply his lips to that ivory skin until Scarlet shuddered and woke and begged him for more. And last night...

Liall smiled and clasped the memory to him, happier than he thought possible. Beside him, Scarlet mumbled and his hips moved, brushing their bodies together, and Liall could feel Scarlet was hard in his sleep, silky erection brushing his thigh. His own greedy sex stirred in response. Oh, that will not do, not at all. If he did not move at once he would never get out of bed. Very gently, Liall disentangled himself from Scarlet's arms and swung his long legs over the side of the high bed.

The Queen had said there would be an opportunity to speak directly to the Baron of Maekva that morning about Cestimir's succession, and Liall could not afford to miss even one chance. Nadiushka insisted that Cestimir, not Vladei, must inherit the throne of Rshan, and Liall had been away from Rshan too long to trust his own judgment on the matter. His mother, on the other hand, had ruled the continent for sixty-three years in his absence. Surely she knew what was best?

Liall drew on a robe and padded into the antechamber,

buried in thought. The meeting was only one of the dozen things he had pressing on him that morning. Another, more isolated issue was the tangle of Scarlet. The Rshani crew on the Ostre Sul had been bad enough, but at least their dislike of Scarlet had been simple. Hate can take many forms. There were those in the palace who would detest Scarlet and wish to harm him because Liall was his lover, or because he was a foreigner and not noble-born, or simply because he was beautiful. There were subtler motivations, too. If Scarlet were harmed, Liall would perhaps be distracted from his purpose, or less dedicated to it in his effort to protect his love. If Scarlet were killed, that, too, would be a warning to Liall. So many dangers to keep watch for.

I should not have allowed him to come, Liall berated himself for the thousandth time. If something terrible happens, I will be to blame.

But oh … last night! Once more, Liall let the memory take him: how Scarlet had been hard and silky against Liall's tongue, the taste of seed flooding his mouth, how the younger man's body had yielded at last, after much careful coaxing, and allowed Liall to penetrate him. The joy of that moment was almost enough to make Liall turn around, march back into the bedroom, and wake him to start over again.

Shall I stop?

Liall had said those words to Scarlet gently, the words sticking in his throat, praying that he would not have to. He wanted Scarlet so much, he nearly shot the first moment he attempted to press inside, which would have spoiled everything. And then Scarlet had sucked on Liall's tongue and spread his legs, so eager and hot and loving and gods he was rising just thinking about it.

They had been lovers in many ways since they first met, and Liall's heart had been lost to Scarlet since the moment he saw the proud red-coat. No, amend that: since Scarlet spoke, and Liall heard something in the young, willful voice that begged an answer of him. Scarlet's fiery spirit stirred a dormant soul that Liall had put to sleep decades ago. Just being near Scarlet made it painfully obvious to Liall that he was incomplete, and finally his own iron will rose up, demanding that the wake and reclaim his life.

Now Liall was like a drunkard, besotted by the feel of Scarlet, forever touching and kissing and holding, barely able to keep his hands to himself. He hoped Scarlet did not tire of it and begin to think him overly lecherous, for Scarlet's opinion of him seemed to be a fey thing at times, apt to change quickly, and it mattered very much to Liall that Scarlet thought well of him. There was not a person in all of Nemerl whose estimation meant more, in Liall's eyes.

Liall's clothes were laid out in the dressing room next to the bath. Thoughtful Nenos had seen to it. He dressed swiftly and slipped into the formal salon nearer the dining room. It was quiet, only the crackle of the fire and the soft hiss of snow on the window behind the heavy, closed draperies.

"Nenos?" Liall called softly. He opened the door between the kitchen and the partitioned dining area, and he saw the old man standing at a counter with his back turned, brewing a pot of che.

"Here, my prince." Nenos's shock of unruly white hair was like a pale nimbus surrounding his head. His skin was a darker brown than Liall's, and he had many creases and merry laugh-lines framing his bright blue eyes. He had a hawkish nose and his jowls were lined with age, but his expression was gentle.

Liall smiled. "And good morning to you, ser."

Nenos flapped a wrinkled hand at him. "None of that with me, my prince. I'm your servant, not your ser, and

I always will be." He turned with a round blue cup of steaming che cradled in his hands. "Here. Drink. You'll need it."

Liall thanked him and drank, enjoying the quiet. "I have much to do today," he said at last. "I cannot be here shut away in a room, and so," he gestured back toward the bedroom where Scarlet was still sleeping, "I must entrust you with a jewel of mine, old friend."

"Oh, dear me. Is that so?" Nenos poured himself a cup. "And this jewel is a troublesome one?"

"Your aged eyes discern much," Liall returned drolly. "Yes, stubborn and willful, with a tendency to wander."

Nenos spared Liall a quick look as he sipped his che. "I shall lock the troublesome jewel in his chambers if I have to, though I do not think he will have much energy to cause mischief this morning. Not after last night."

Liall was horrified to feel a blush creeping across his cheeks. Nenos had heard them. Of course. Half the Nauhinir probably heard them. Liall ducked his head. "If your sleep was disturbed, I—"

Nenos chuckled.

"It is all very well for you to tease. You have had a wife for ninety years."

"Ninety-two."

"Pardon me."

They grinned at each other and drank their che.

"You know," Nenos continued as he stacked the che utensils in the basin, to be carried away with the other dishes to the great kitchens below in the palace. "I have had much experience with willful young men who don't know how to stay put." His old eyes met Liall's for a moment, and there was a mist over his gaze. "I do not think I have said how good it is to see you again, Nazheradei."

Liall bowed his head over his cup. "I did not mean to

abandon so many. I had no choice. You know that."

Nenos quickly looked away to hide any emotion.

"Your *che* is getting cold," he said gruffly.

Liall took another sip. It was stronger than most Byzan blends. He had missed it, and Nenos. Probably one of the few people he would ever miss from Rshan. "You never did find me that day," Liall said suddenly, a hint of a teasing smile on his lips.

The old man huffed in amusement. "I would never have found you the next time either, if Nadei hadn't…"

Nenos trailed off, his face falling into lines of sorrow.

"Forgive me, my prince. It was an accident. I did not mean to speak of him."

"There's nothing to forgive." The cup was clenched hard in Liall's hands. Liall put it in the basin before he broke it, mindful of Nenos's regretful expression. "Thank you for the *che*," he murmured, before leaving the kitchen and pulling the door closed softly.

Liall could have walked through the Nauhinir and gotten to the Queen's tier faster, but his nerves were raw. He did not feel like ignoring stares or pretending to ignore them in the palace corridors, and there would be many today. Exiting the palace through the enclosed north gardens, he turned east toward the stables, passing the Shining Tower, where the death knell tolls for fallen kings and one day would toll for his mother. From there, he planned to cut back through the greenhouse and thence the kitchen and into the stairs, where he was unlikely to cross paths with anyone this time of day. His assumption was that there had been no structural changes to the palace in the last sixty years, and in this, he was correct.

The stables smelled of dung, sweet hay, sawdust and healthy, well-tended animals. A few soldiers milled about, and there were guards and grooms as well, but they were busy at their own tasks. After the first disbelieving stares and whispers, they spared Liall little attention. Walking briskly through the vast, vaulted building, he spied in a line of tethered horses a blue-black stallion that was a hand higher than the rest. The mount was caparisoned in silver with a bridle made of strong blue silk, tough as leather. Liall stopped and ran his hand through the mount's thick mane, marveling at the softness. The stallion whinnied and gave Liall a knowing look from his dark, wet eyes, and a bolt of recognition hit the prince.

"You can't be... *Argent?* Oh Deva, you can't be."

"He is not, but Argent was his grandsire."

Liall turned at the voice, and his jaw dropped. "Jarek!"

"Hello, *iaresh.*"

Khatai Jarek, the Queen's Champion, whom her younger recruits affectionately referred to as the Lion. The title *khatai* is like a general, one who leads the armies, and she was a few inches taller than Liall. Her hair – she still gathered it in a thick braid on her neck, Liall saw – had gone to gray, and there were new lines around her beautiful indigo eyes and her generous mouth, but her smile was the same. His heart leapt when she simply gathered him up in her great arms, muddied and burdened as she was with armor and weapons, and hugged him fiercely. It was like being fifteen again. He was so startled and pleased to see her that when she laughingly drew back and cupped his face in her rough hands, Liall grinned foolishly at her and pounded her shoulder. Perhaps she took it for encouragement, for she tugged her face forward and kissed him full on the mouth, somewhat longer than was proper even for old friends. When she released Liall, he almost scurried backwards. She laughed again.

"I was happy to see you. Please do not take offense, my prince." She sketched a short and choppy bow: a soldier's obeisance.

Liall made a noise of disgust. "Stop. There has never been any of that between us. I am glad to see you, too."

"You've arrived just in time."

Jarek always was predictably to the point. "The army has not been called out yet, surely?"

She looked around quickly, her eyes darting to the corners. "Not here," she said lowly. "Follow me."

Jarek was housed in a solitary, guarded room next to the large and bustling soldier's barracks upwind of the stables. She waved away the soldier who stood post by her door and motioned Liall to come in, and then stripped off her gloves and tossed them to her waiting aide, a young, pretty man who discreetly stepped out. There were maps unrolled on her desk and a crude, scaled model of the Nauhinir Palace. "Wine?" she asked.

"Che, if you have it."

"We do." She snapped her fingers and her aide reappeared. He was a young soldier with the braided hair of the northern clans, and he had a red scar over the bridge of his nose that marred his pretty looks a little.

"Me'em?"

"Bring us che, Yveny. Not the grass-squeezings they serve the troops either."

"Aye, me'em."

Yveny ducked out, off to find the che. Liall gave Jarek a knowing look which she returned blandly.

"There are many rewards to risking your life for the Queen, such as handsome young men who do not simper at sharing the bed of a khatai," she said.

Liall bit his tongue on the reply that rose. No. Best to

leave that bit of personal history to rumor and memory. Liall traced his fingers on the map, drawing a line from Fanorl to Na Karmun. There were other maps, most notably ones of Uzna Minor, Vladei and his brother Eleferi's province, and Jadizek, who owed its hereditary loyalty to Shikhoza's family.

"Are these coincidences?"

She snorted as she poured wine for herself. "You know me better than that."

Liall sighed. "This goes all the way to the eastern shore of Kalas Nauhin, I see."

"You see clearly. Vladei has been making preparation for this time since the day Cestimir was born. The apple has rotted deep, my prince."

"What will you do?"

She shrugged. "I will obey my Queen, and put a halt to them. The distaff line of Druz, your mother's house, ruled here for a thousand years before your father's. Cestimir's claim through his mother's bloodline is ten times as valid as Vladei's, whose claim stems from your uncle, the half-royal. Yet," she finished sourly, "we must thank your father's half-brother, for without him we would not have Cestimir."

"Did my mother see Lankomir that way?" Liall asked sharply. "As a stud to serve the line of Druz?"

"She is a prudent ruler," the khatai evaded, which was answer enough.

"Jarek..."

She gave him a long, measuring look. "Nadiushka is a Queen first. Second, she is Rshani. Third, a mother. Last, if ever, she may have leisure to be a woman, but I do not believe she has given thought to that in a long time. She has Bhakamir, who reminds her that she is a woman sometimes, though even he knows she is well past such pleasures."

Nadiushka had never liked Lankomi, and Liall had marveled when the news came to him in Byzantur that she had consented to marry him, yet now many things were clear. Her dead husband's half-brother had been a scantling, used only to provide an heir for Rshan that held claim from both houses. Whatever else Nadiushka might have felt in her secret heart, publicly she declared for Rshan first, herself after. A throb of sympathy and guilt passed through Liall: How utterly alone I left her. How abandoned she must have felt, and angry.

He did not press Jarek further on the matter, turning instead back to the maps. "Is there a plan?"

"When is there ever not? Uzna has been a breeding ground for unrest for the past two centuries. Now these vermin, these rebels loyal to Vladei," she stabbed a finger at the maps of Magur and Uzna Minor "have taken hold here and they must be stamped out. An example will have to be made."

That alarmed Liall. "Of whom?"

Jarek drank the small cup of wine in one swallow and wiped her mouth with her hand. "Not who, what. Magur."

"Oh," he said with sarcasm. "And there are no people in Magur, I gather."

"There are, but not very many and we can't afford to think of them as people. Magur is a thing that threatens the safety of the empire, so Magur must go. It's a town, not a city like Uzna or Jadizek, so the outcry among the nobles will be small. The routing will not be tied to this business of Vladei and his claim to the throne, not publicly. We will blame it on failure to pay taxes and inciting the garrison there to disaffect, which will fool no one. But... we will get our message out loud and clear: challenge further, and regret."

Liall nodded, though his gut clenched with distaste.

Jarek knew her business. Far be it from him to dictate to a general the affairs on her own field. He had learned his lesson on that account. "You never change," he said.

"All people change." Jarek loosened her armor and laid her sword across the narrow bunk. "You have." Then she grinned. "Where is that delicate prince who traipsed into my unit, fresh from the palace, wanting to learn to be soldier? Eh, you were so soft I could still see the silk cushion attached to your ass."

They laughed together. It was more than a little true. "I was fifteen, what did you want?"

"Oh, a legend at the very least. That's what you thought anyway."

"The Tribeland campaigns taught me better," Liall chuckled, and then sobered a little. It was not funny. Those brutal campaigns had stripped away the youth in him, left him feel burned in his soul and hurting for years, and Jarek had been there to see it.

Jarek waved her hand. "Ah, lad, that was so long ago. Look at you now."

His mouth curved as he hitched one leg up to sit on her desk and folded his arms. "What do you see, I wonder?"

"Well, not a *lion*," she said, which made him smile again. "Or a snow bear, but a wolf at the very least. I hear you are almost a legend among the lenilyn." Jarek stepped closer to him, her eyes growing hard. "Let me look at you for a moment."

After a full minute of searching Liall's face, she nodded shortly as if satisfied with the silent answer she had gained. "You're a good man, Nazir. I'm glad to see it."

Liall looked away, shaken. "I am not always so good."

"Here now." Jarek's hand was under his chin, making him look at her. "You were always expecting more from yourself than any five men could give," She shook her head, and her hand turned caressing. "Iaresh," she said lowly. Beauty. "You're enough to make a woman lose her head and do foolish things."

His heart was beating very fast. Oh, this was too much like being a boy again, which he did not think he truly enjoyed, but the feeling was compelling, her hands holding him still as her fingers began to explore the lines of his face gently.

"Like what?" Liall asked against all sense and reason, his throat dry.

"Like this."

She kissed him. Jarek had always had a rude tongue, but Liall was unprepared for the way she jerked him forward and sealed her mouth over his, how her tongue forced its way so quickly past his lips and plunged almost to the entrance of his throat, then slowed to learn his mouth again, to map every inch of it with fluttering softness as her skin brushed his cheek and her teeth nipped at his lower lip.

Gods, that tongue. He remembered the first time she had bedded him – for that's the way it was; she bedded him, not the other way around – and they had been lying in her bunk and touching. Liall was a fresh recruit in the khatai's tent, and she was pleasuring him with her hand, calling him beauty, iaresh, stroking his nude body with a skill that made him shudder and writhe and call out in a voice that shamed him to remember later.

Liall had seen her wield a sword and thought she was a demon with a blade, but that skill was only matched by her lovemaking. Scarlet had evinced surprise that he was such a good lover. Well, here is where he learned it.

Only when her hand dropped to settle between Liall's legs did he pull back. "Stop! I..." he gasped, and shook his head, "I regret, but I cannot."

She smiled but did not remove her hand. "The little one? I heard you brought back an outlander concubine."

"Not concubine. Scarlet is my t'aishka."

He had not thought it was possible to surprise her. "I believed that part was exaggeration: servant's gossip or idle tales. Is he truly your forever beloved, this peasant lenilyn?"

"His name is Scarlet."

"Yes, I heard you." Her hand cupped and caressed him, and he could not hold back a hiss of pleasure as his flesh came alive under her touch, stiffening quickly.

Hells, what was this? He was not a boy to be seduced, he was a man. A man who has just left his lover's bed, he thought with a flush of shame. At least, I was a man before I walked into her room. The past has such power over us.

Liall firmly put his hand over Jarek's and pulled it away. "Jarek, I cannot."

She paused. After a moment, she nodded and stepped back from him. "As you wish. I would never force myself on you."

She said this last in such a strange way that it made him ache. "Nor did you ever," Liall said fervently. "I cherish our memories, but that was long ago."

She looked away from him and shrugged, making light of it. She grinned again. "Well, I knew that, but it was just so good to see you."

"And I, you," Liall said sincerely.

They were silent for a moment, and Jarek busied herself with finding a fresh cloak from her clothing chest. Liall wiped his mouth and tried to still the frantic beating of his heart.

"Does he know?"

"Hm? Who?"

"The lenilyn. Scarlet. Does he know?"

Liall frowned. "What do you mean? He does not know about us, I did not even know you were here until I saw Argent."

"No." She seemed distant. "Not about us. Does he know about Nadei?"

Oh. His hands clasped together of their own accord.

"He... suspects something is being withheld from him."

"Ah." Jarek threw a fresh cloak around her shoulders and buckled it. "And what will you do when your t'aishka discovers the manner of your exile and the circumstances surrounding it?"

He felt like shouting. How could she bring this up now, and why? "You are trying to wound me," Liall accused.

"I'm trying to spare you pain," she shot back. "I'm a soldier, and a soldier says goodbye to too many friends in life, not to mention lovers and husbands. Hilurin are... They are not us, Nazir. They're a rigid and ignorant people, and they don't think the same."

Liall bowed his head. Ancient prejudices cannot be dismissed with a word, and to recite all he had learned about Byzans in the last sixty years would have taken all day. The matter needed a long explanation or none, so he kept silent.

"Have you explained the facts to him?"

"No," Liall answered coldly, "He does not know, and he will not know. As you said, Hilurin are a rigid people. There is no room in Scarlet's honor for what I have done. He would leave me."

"And how would he do that?" Jarek returned reasonably. "He is at your mercy here, yours to do with as you wish. He can't go anywhere at all without your consent."

"He will leave me in his heart."

"When lying would so endear you."

"Cease this!" Liall shouted at last, rising from his

chair with his fists clenched. "What am I to tell him? That I murdered my own brother?"

In the long silence that followed, Jarek sighed and looked away. "Those were your words, not mine, my prince. But I do suggest you tell Scarlet about Nadei as quickly as possible, before he finds out on his own. It's a terrible thing to be deceived by the ones closest to you, Nazir. He may forgive your past. The present is another matter."

So saying, she walked to the door. "Yveny will be back with the che soon," she murmured, and closed the door behind her. Liall could hear the muffled thump of her boot heels as she strode away.

"Do you forgive me, Jarek?" Liall whispered to the empty room.

-end-

To be concluded in Scarlet and the White Wolf, Book 3: The Land of Night.

Author's Bio

Kirby Crow worked as an entertainment editor and ghostwriter for several years before happily giving it up to bake more brownies, read more yaoi, play more video games, and write her own novels.

Changing weather patterns, watering bans, and pesticides have unhappily forced her to give up growing roses, alas.

Her published novels are **Prisoner of the Raven** (historical romance, Torquere Press, 2005), **Scarlet and the White Wolf: The Pedlar and the Bandit King** (fantasy romance, Torquere Press, 2006), **Mariner's Luck** (fantasy romance, Torquere Press, 2007), and **The Land of Night** (fantasy romance, Torquere Press, 2007). They are available from Torquere Books, most online book retailers, and Amazon.

Kirby is a Spectrum Book Awards nominee, and is hard at work on two more fantasy novels and one horror novel, to be announced on her website. http://kirbycrow.com